DEIMOS

CUPID'S CAPTIVE, BOOK THREE

Eva Pohler

Eva Pohler Books
20011 Park Ranch
San Antonio, Texas 78259
www.evapohler.com

Book Layout ©2017 BookDesignTemplates.com

Book Cover Design by Keri Knutson

Deimos/ Eva Pohler. -- 1st ed.
Paperback ISBN: 978-1-958390-63-4

I want you, Phobos. But I also want Deimos.

—ELLIE

Contents

For my husband.

Hecate's Vision

Ellie lay on the couch in the moon goddess's cave on Mont Forel, fighting tears. Deimos sat beside her, stroking her arm, as she stared into the fire blazing in the hearth. Hecate slept on a couch opposite them, paralyzed from Zeus's lightning bolt. Rhythmic snores echoed throughout the dark cave, but they weren't Hecate's; they came from deeper in the mountain, where Selene's lover slept.

"Only the Fates know for certain what the future holds," Deimos said, trying to reassure her.

But Ellie could not be reassured.

"Hecate said that her visions sometimes change," he added, raking his hand through his vibrant red hair. "Apollo has said the same."

Ellie clutched her belly as tears fell from her eyes. She'd barely had time to process the news that she was having twin girls, much less the vision of doom from Hecate.

"I won't let anything happen to you or the babies," Deimos said. "I promise."

Ellie knew he meant what he said. She also knew it was a promise he couldn't keep.

Zeus and the loyalists had been desperate to imprison Ellie. If they got wind of this new vision, they would never allow the twins to be born.

Before she'd been paralyzed, Hecate had revealed to Deimos and to the other rebels a recurring vision that had plagued her in recent days. In her vision, the gods were gathered in the great hall on Mount Olympus. Ellie was there with her two little girls. Mount Olympus became bathed in darkness. The mountain shook. The gods gasped and glanced around in horror. The floor of the great hall cracked in half and, as the mountain fell—and the temple along with it—many of the gods fell, too. They fell into the crevice and down into the depths of the mountain, where Gaia—Mother Earth—was waiting with her mouth wide open.

Zeus and Hera were among those who fell. Hecate had been unable to identify everyone who was lost or who remained standing on what was left of the rubble of Mount Olympus. However, she did see among the survivors Ellie, Deimos, and one—only one—of Ellie's twins. The other had fallen, along with Phobos, into the deep abyss and had been swallowed by the darkness.

When Ellie had asked if this meant the end was at least a year away, since her babies were *standing* in the vision, Deimos had shaken his head.

"Gods age differently from humans and from one another. Most age quickly in childhood and then, at adolescence, age so slowly that they seem not to age at all."

"What about pregnancy?" she'd asked. "Is it nine months, like it is for mortals?"

"It's different for every goddess."

Ellie had bit her lip until it had bled. "We could have mere *days*. That's what you're saying."

"I'm afraid so."

She had never felt so hopeless, so full of despair. She was the goddess of lost causes, and yet she could do nothing to help herself.

Now, she closed her eyes. The prayers to her from Phobos broke her heart. He prayed: *Please don't do anything stupid that might jeopardize you and the babies. You can be pigheaded, Ellie. You know you can. Just don't forget about me down here, okay? Deimos may be good looking—damned good looking, it's true. But he's too stuffy for you. Professor Deimos doesn't know how to make you laugh— at least, not as well as I do. Oh, gods, maybe he challenges your mind in ways I can't—or won't. Fuck, Ellie. Maybe you're better off with Deimos.*

By the way, tell Deimos that Aphrodite erased Jaquelyn's memory of the time she overheard us talking about the gods. The girl is blissfully ignorant again.

"Ellie?" Deimos asked, his crystal blue eyes full of concern.

"I want to sleep."

He stroked her cheek. "Good. Get some rest."

He leaned over and touched his lips to hers as he tucked a quilt around her.

Ellie didn't care about rest. She only wanted to stop thinking and feeling and hearing the many prayers that came to her from all over the world. There were so many desperate people praying for their lost causes. Businesses were going under, families were getting evicted, and some weren't sure where they'd get their next meal. But what could Ellie do when her own life and the lives of her babies were in danger?

Sleep would be a welcome escape.

Then, for the first time, she heard a prayer from her mother: *Ellie, where are you? It's a week before Christmas, and I ain't heard nothing from you, child. You don't answer your phone. You stopped sending postcards. For all I know you could be dead.*

"My poor Mama," Ellie whispered. "She's worried sick."

"We'll get word to her as soon as we can," Deimos said. "Now stop worrying and get some rest."

Please, Hypnos, she prayed. *Bring me sleep.*

Deimos carefully extricated himself from the couch, where he'd been sitting beside the sleeping Ellie with her legs draped over his lap. He'd watched her sleep for half an hour, praying to all the gods in the rebellion to protect her and the babies. Now, he needed to stretch his legs and to think. He paced before the fire. He felt like a caged animal at the mercy of his captors, even though he was hiding in the cave by choice.

For six weeks, he'd had to endure watching the love of his life with his brother on the west Texas ranch. Although Deimos had taken comfort in Ellie's prayers to him, he'd come to realize something: Ellie would never choose.

It would almost be cruel to make her do so.

He'd wrestled with the idea of letting her go and had even convinced himself that he would—that it was the right thing to do, if he really loved her. But the moment she was in his arms again, he knew he couldn't do it—not to himself or to her. They needed one another. They belonged together.

After holding her in his arms again, he truly believed that, if he walked away to spare her from having to choose, she'd be miserable without him. And he knew the same would be true if she gave up his brother.

Ellie was waiting to let the paternity of her babies decide, but Deimos knew in his heart that it didn't matter—not because he believed in Hecate's vision, but because he believed Ellie would *always* love Phobos as much as she loved him.

When Hecate had shared her vision with the rebellion in the throne room of the Underworld, Artemis had said something to Deimos that had upset him. She'd said, "It looks like you get the girl in the end."

It had taken every bit of his self-control not to berate her. Instead, he'd taken a deep breath and had asked, "Do you really think I'd pay such a price?"

Artemis had glared at him with her forest-green eyes. "Watch your tone! I was only kidding."

"Some gods are more than willing to throw their brothers, sons, and daughters to the wolves," Hades had said. "You can't blame Artemis for believing you to be one of them."

"I was only kidding," Artemis had said again.

Persephone had placed her slender arm around her husband's waist. "Let's get back to the plan, darling. What are we going to do?"

"I've said from the beginning—when Apollo first brought this talk of a reckoning to our attention—that we gods are being judged. If we want to come out of this unscathed, we must, no matter how bad things get, take the high moral ground."

Deimos had found those words to be ironic, considering that Hades had once been accused of attempting to kill one of his children while it was still in the womb, but Deimos had held his tongue.

Artemis had raised her bow. "We protect Ellie."

"And her babies," Hermes had added.

"At all cost," Hephaestus had said.

Hypnos and Thanatos had agreed.

"I believe that's the only hope we have of saving ourselves," Hades had said.

For the members of the rebellion, saving Ellie and her babies meant saving themselves; for Deimos, it was about love. It wasn't the arrow of love or the arrow of hate driving him; the two arrows had canceled each other out. This was his *heart*, which had come to care for another more than he'd ever thought possible. He would fight to protect Ellie from Zeus and the loyalists, and, if Hecate's vision came to be, he would do everything in his power to save his brother and Ellie's child—a child that he felt, deep in his soul, belonged to him, too.

Ellie stirred. When her eyes sought his across the room, Deimos grinned. She returned his smile, filling his heart with everything good. Her smile vanquished the anxiety that had taken over his thoughts. He flew to her and knelt by her side.

"I was dreaming about you," she whispered.

"A good dream, I hope."

"*Very* good."

"Thank you, Hypnos."

"Can I have a kiss?"

Deimos cradled her head and brought her mouth to his. He closed his eyes and breathed in her scent, licked her lips to enjoy her taste. Then he caressed her check before sliding his hand to her throat, her chest. Her heart pounded beneath his fingertips as he deepened his kiss and cupped her breast.

"Oh, Deimos," she whispered against his lips.

"I want you so badly," he whispered back.

"You can have me," she said.

Deimos glanced over at Hecate, who was still sleeping, before he tugged off his shirt and helped Ellie out of hers. They scrambled from their shoes and pants before he climbed beside her on the couch, his chest against her breasts. With his hands on her lower back, he pressed her against him. She rubbed herself against his thigh, sending shocks of desire through every muscle in his body. His hands sought her bottom before he whipped her around, putting himself beneath her. She sat up and straddled him, with her knees on either side of him. Her breasts dangled over him as she lifted her bottom and found him waiting for that hot, moist spot. She guided him and moaned with pleasure as he entered.

Deimos tried to be quiet, so as not to wake the others sleeping in the cave, but his efforts were in vain. The intense pleasure he felt, as Ellie raised and lowered herself, found a way to his throat, and he gasped and moaned until he exploded with ecstasy.

Ellie collapsed against him. He smoothed her hair and kissed her shoulder.

As much as he wanted to lie there, skin against skin, for however long they wished, Deimos knew Selene would soon return. He sat up and held Ellie on his lap as he kissed her once more. Then he said, "We better get dressed."

"Don't do it on my account," Selene said from the entrance to her cave, her luminous long hair and robe billowing in the breeze. She sat in her chariot, smirking.

"Selene!" Deimos pulled the quilt from the floor and wrapped it around Ellie, while he used his powers to instantly dress them. "I didn't hear you arrive."

"Obviously." She climbed from the chariot and unbridled her horses. "But don't mind me. I'm going to bed. Maybe I'll make love to Endymion first, now that you've got me in the mood."

Ellie climbed from Deimos's lap and sat beside him with crimson cheeks.

"I thought you said that your wards are weakest on the new moon, while you sleep," Deimos pointed out. "Should I stand guard?"

"No," she said. "I put up extra protections yesterday. No one will get past them."

Just then Hermes appeared, holding the helm of invisibility. "I wouldn't go so far as to say *that.*"

"Hermes!" Deimos gawked. "How long have you been there beneath the helm?"

Hermes's cheeks turned nearly as red as Ellie's. "Er, not long."

Deimos glanced at Ellie who wouldn't meet his eyes. She curled the quilt around her and stared at the fire in the hearth.

It was one thing to know that gods could see through clothes and buildings and so forth, but it was another to know that they'd been right there in the room with you during your most vulnerable moment.

"Why have you come?" Selene asked.

Hermes wore a scabbard and shield that Deimos had never seen before. "Well, you see, I went to return the helm to Lord Hades, and he told me to deliver it to Ellie."

Ellie looked up at Hermes with wide eyes. "To me? Why?"

"He knew you'd return to Phobos."

Deimos jumped to his feet. "Even with the helm, that would be risky."

Hermes handed the helm to Ellie. "True. But now you have options."

"Thank you," Ellie said.

Hermes removed the scabbard and shield and handed them to Ellie. "Hephaestus made these for you. Deimos can show you how to use and to conjure them."

"To what?" Ellie looked up at Deimos. She had the weapons draped across the quilt on her lap.

"I'll explain later," Deimos assured her. Then, he asked Hermes, "Any updates?"

"I'm going to bed," Selene said. "You can catch me up later." Then, to her horses, she said, "Come on, ladies. To your stalls."

Selene flew to the back of the cave, where her lover was sleeping. Her mares followed.

"Not much to report," Hermes said as he scratched his curly black head. "Hephaestus is still working on Athena. I expect they'll set up a meeting with her soon."

Deimos gnawed on his lower lip. Athena was unpredictable. He feared approaching her would backfire.

Hermes crossed the room to where Hecate lay. He touched her cheek.

She opened her eyes and smiled up at him. Her black and white hair lay in long strands across her pillow.

"You can move your mouth," Hermes said. "That's progress."

"I'm thirsty," she said.

Hermes found a goblet on the table beside the couch and gently lifted Hecate's head while she drank.

"Thank you," she said when she'd finished.

"How do you feel?" Hermes asked.

"Stiff."

Hermes took a seat on the couch with Hecate's feet in his lap. "Maybe if we get your blood flowing." He massaged her stockinged feet.

"I wish I could feel that," Hecate said.

"You'll be good as new before long, Hecate." Deimos returned to his seat beside Ellie.

"Are *you* having visions now?" she teased.

"I wish," Deimos said with a laugh.

"No, you don't," Hecate said. "I wouldn't wish them on anyone. It's a curse, especially when there's rarely anything to be done about them."

"You said there's a chance," Deimos said, not wanting to add to Ellie's despair.

"There's always a chance," she said. "However slight."

"When can we get a message to Phobos?" Ellie asked. "I can't imagine how hard it must be on him, to not know what's going on."

"I'd like to watch over Hecate while you're gone," Hermes said. "Assuming you're going with her, Deimos."

Deimos gaped for a moment. "Uh, we can't go *now*. Ellie doesn't know how to use her powers. She needs some training before we attempt something that dangerous."

"Agreed," Hermes said. "Summon me when you're ready."

Hermes vanished.

Ellie pulled her sword from its jeweled scabbard. "Are you really going to teach me how to use these things?"

"Of course," he said. "You have a lot to learn, so we better get started."

CHAPTER TWO

Goddess in Training

Ellie had been sparring with Deimos for hours in Selene's cave, maneuvering around the couches, the wooden table and chairs, and the chariot, which Selene had parked at the mouth of the cave. Selene's two silver horses fed on hay in their stalls further in the mountain, and Ellie had been promised a chance to see them if she satisfied Deimos with her swordsmanship.

She missed the horses on the Garcia ranch more than she'd ever thought possible.

"Elbows out," Deimos said.

She stepped back and did as he instructed.

"Widen your stance and shift your weight…that's it."

"Can we see the horses now?" she asked.

"I want you to incorporate flight and god-travel more frequently."

Ellie vanished and reappeared behind Deimos with her sword at his throat. "Now?"

He dropped his sword to his side and turned to her with a smirk. "Fine. But let me see you conjure your weapons once more."

Ellie sheathed her sword and focused on sending it and her shield to the couch, where she'd been lying earlier. Then she conjured them back, so that they were strapped onto her body—shield across her shoulders like a backpack and scabbard belted around her hips.

"Nice," Deimos said. "Put them back on the couch, and we'll go see the horses."

She did as she was told, grateful to finally have a break.

"Let's fly. Shall we?" Deimos suggested.

She supposed the practice was good for her.

Selene's cave was tall with silver stalactites hanging, like crystals, from the ceiling. They looked hard and sharp but were moist and mushy on the ends. The sound of running water echoed against the walls the further back into the cave they flew. It was also darker—though, with god vision, darkness wasn't a problem for Ellie.

They flew past Selene sleeping beside her lover on a feather mattress in a nook to one side as they followed the tunnel deeper into the mountain. Ellie smelled the scent of hay and manure as they reached the stalls—which were more like grottos, as they had no gates.

"Hello, there," Ellie said softly, so as not to wake the others.

"This is Crescent," Deimos said as he stroked the silver mane of the horse to their left. "And that one is Luna."

The horses seemed to become apprehensive in their presence.

"I'll leave you to them," Deimos said. "I can see I have an effect on them."

Left alone with the horses, Ellie thought only of Phobos and how worried he must be. His last words, before he'd been taken from Mount Olympus, were of the babies. He'd asked Hera if they were his. But Hera had refused to answer him.

Ellie hoped the animals on the ranch kept him distracted. She wondered if Deimos the cat was still around, or if Julio and Iglesias had chased him off. What of Bailey, Blondie, Gypsy, Sherlock, and Chestnut? Did they bring Phobos comfort, as Crescent and Luna were doing for Ellie now? He hadn't mentioned them in his prayers. His words to Ellie had been full of condemnation of himself, of where he'd gone wrong as a friend and a lover. He seemed resigned to let Deimos have her.

Why had he given up on her so quickly?

The more she thought about it, the more she wondered if he were protecting his heart. He was terrified of losing her—either because of some disaster that would be orchestrated by Zeus and the loyalists or because she would choose Deimos. He'd convinced himself that she was better off with Deimos, to soften the blow he believed was coming in one form or another.

It was typical of him to run from his feelings rather than to face them. It was why he preferred novels and jokes to nonfiction and serious conversation.

Deimos had once accused Ellie of being the same way. He'd said she ran from her unresolved issues. He'd said that her relationships with her mother and sister were fractured and, rather than repairing them, Ellie had left. He'd said, "You love your mother, but you hate her too, and you hate that you hate her, because you know she doesn't deserve it."

Now that she felt Phobos doing the same thing to her—letting her go rather than facing their unresolved issues—she knew what it felt like to be on the other side, and it hurt. Had she hurt her mother in the same way? Ellie's stomach clenched.

She wished Phobos could hear her prayers. If he could, she'd tell him that she was safe, for the moment, and missing him. She'd say that she couldn't stand being away from him. She'd tell him that she loved him, ached for him, needed him.

And she'd say that everything was going to be okay.

She'd say this knowing that everything was not going to be okay.

Deimos was as anxious as Ellie to pay his brothers a visit. He'd hated the look on their faces as their mother returned them to the ranch to finish out their sentences. It was the look of utter helplessness. He knew how it felt to be stripped of one's powers and cut off from the rest of the gods. That feeling of helplessness was worse than any pain Deimos had experienced.

He was tempted to take the helm and to fly to the ranch without Ellie, to keep her safe; however, he knew it would hurt and anger her. She wanted more than to reassure Phobos that she was safe. She wanted to see him.

He checked on Hecate and found her sleeping. He filled a goblet with wine and sat on the couch to drink and to wait for Ellie. Then he had an idea: before flying with the helm to the Garcia ranch, they would practice by flying to a different destination, and he knew just the one.

He finished his wine, grabbed the helm, and flew to the stalls, where Ellie was brushing Luna.

"I'm nearly done," Ellie said. "Crescent was so happy when I found the brush and gave her a good grooming, and now Luna is practically purring. Look at her face."

"Have you ever heard of the aurora borealis?"

"The northern lights?"

"Exactly. How'd you like to see them, in person?"

She smiled up at him "Seriously?"

He showed her the helm "For practice."

"Let's do it."

"Once we leave this cave, we can't speak a word or make a sound. The helm will make us invisible to even the gods, but our sounds will carry. You understand?"

Ellie returned the horse brush to a ledge. "Yes, professor."

Deimos chuckled and shook his head. "We'll communicate telepathically, through prayer."

Fine, she prayed. *Can you hear me?*

He ignored her, as a trick.

Deimos, can you hear me? There's a place in France where the naked ladies dance. There's a hole in the wall where the men can see it all.

Deimos had to work hard not to laugh. "Why don't we practice telepathic communication before we fly off?"

"You mean you couldn't hear me just then?"

"Hear what?"

"Oh, no! Deimos, I suck!"

Laughing, he sang, "There's a place in France where the naked ladies dance."

She punched his arm. "That was mean."

"Come on," he said. "Goodbye, Crescent. Goodbye, Luna."

"Goodbye," Ellie said as he led her from the stalls.

They flew past the sleeping moon goddess and her lover, over the table and chairs, and over the chariot to the mouth of the cave.

"*You* should wear the helm, in case we get separated," Deimos said, handing it over to her.

"Okay." She placed it onto her head and vanished.

He chuckled. "You do recall that we have to be touching for me to see you."

When she made no reply, he reached out for her. "Ellie?"

His hand passed through air. He brought up the other and turned in a circle, flailing his arms. "Ellie? This isn't funny."

He was about to go into full-blown panic mode when he felt her lips against his. He encircled her waist and returned her smile.

"Never do that again," he said.

"Fine. If you don't want a kiss."

He pulled her into him and swept his mouth against hers, gently tantalizing her, to be sure she knew that wasn't what he meant.

She purred in his arms.

"I suppose we don't have to leave right away," he said near her ear.

"I'd feel too guilty," she whispered, "delaying our message to Phobos, who must be out of his mind with worry, while we enjoyed ourselves. Seeing the northern lights seems selfish enough already."

Deimos cleared his throat and straightened his back. "You're right. Let's go."

He took her hand and pulled her into the frosty air, among snow-capped mountaintops. She wobbled, kicked her legs, and tightened her grip, as if she'd forgotten her power of flight.

"Whoa!" she cried.

You've got this, he said. *Remember not to make a sound.*

I'm sorry. I didn't realize how high we were.

Not for long. And we don't have far to go.

Where are we going?

Out of these mountains, where we can get a better view. See there? That's Baffin Bay. Once we're out of these clouds, we may have a view of the lights.

They descended toward the snow-covered coast of Greenland, outside of a small village, where there wouldn't be clouds or light pollution interfering with their view.

They could see the streaks of color before they'd landed on their feet.

Oh, my. This is incredible, Ellie prayed.

Do you know why they call it the aurora borealis?

Ellie shook her head.

Aurora is the name the Romans call Eos—Dawn. And Borealis comes from the northern wind, Boreas.

So many colors, she said. *I can't decide whether I like the green or the purple best.*

As the sun rotates, it creates sunspots that hurl solar wind into space. They take about forty hours to get here. When they collide with oxygen in our atmosphere, they make green and yellow. When they collide with nitrogen, they make the pinks and purples.

What makes them dance? she asked.

The stronger the solar flare, the more the colors change and give the appearance of dancing.

Breathtaking. Absolutely breathtaking.

He turned to her and cupped her face. *As are you.*

She covered her mouth to stifle a giggle.

He tried not to look hurt as he grinned. *Too cheesy? You know, there's a fine line between cheese and grand romantic gesture.*

She threw her arms around his neck. *This is the grandest romantic gesture ever. Thank you.*

They stood there in a tight embrace and gazed up at the moving lights for a few more minutes before Deimos asked, *Shall we return to the cave and make a plan?*

Ellie nodded and kissed his cheek. *Ready when you are.*

First, let me see you conjure your sword and shield.

He'd barely finished the prayer to her, when her shield and scabbard appeared on her body.

Excellent, he said. *Want to practice flying with them?*

Good idea.

Hand in hand, they ascended into the sky and flew toward the mountains on the east side of Greenland. Once they were in the clouds, the northern lights were no longer visible.

Hey, Ellie said. *Do you think we can stop by Louisiana on the way back from Texas? I haven't seen my family in ages. I'd just like to look in on them and make sure they're okay—maybe leave them a note.*

I suppose so. Phobos and I were supposed to be sending postcards to your mother from around the world, but we've been a bit tied up.

Ellie covered her mouth to stifle her laugh.

Perhaps we should go now, Deimos suggested. *To give you more practice.*

Can we?

Just be careful. I doubt a loyalist will be watching your childhood home, but you can never be too careful.

Ellie held onto Deimos's hand as they turned back toward Baffin Bay and headed southwest, toward America. She was amazed by how clear everything appeared to her below. As they flew over the bay, she could see several feet beneath the icy water, where colorful marine animals scurried about, living their lives. As Ellie and Deimos crossed over Canada, she noticed cars and people moving among the buildings in patterns that were surprisingly like those of the sea animals.

Amid the many prayers about lost causes came another from her Mom: *My daughter is a lost cause. If you can hear me, lawd, please help.*

Dominique can't afford another baby. What are we gonna do? How we gonna afford diapers and baby food? Will I lose my housing if they find out we have more than three living here? Dominique won't have an abortion. She thinks the daddy will marry her once she's had two of his kids. And when he don't, will she have three? Lawd, help her. Why she want that baby daddy so badly? She longs for the perfect little family. Is it because she never knew her father? Should I have told Benny and allowed him into her life, even though he was trouble? Is this my fault? Did I do this to her? Help me, lawd. I'm about to lose my mind.

Ellie wasn't sure what she could do to help her mother and sister, but she had to try.

When they flew over Louisiana to the east part of New Orleans, to the Lower Ninth Ward, Ellie felt a pang of homesickness. It had been nearly a year since she'd gone home—since last Christmas. She wondered if she'd even recognize Jonivan.

They landed on the roof of Ellie's house as the sun was setting. Morning had arrived in Greenland, but not in New Orleans. And although it was warmer and muggier here, Ellie felt unaffected by the climate change. It was a bizarre feeling.

Her three-bedroom, one-bath house seemed enormous compared to the shack she'd lived in for three months in west Texas, but it wasn't much larger than the bedroom suite she'd lived in at Cupid and Psyche's castle. Growing up, she hadn't realized how poor they were. Her friends were poor, too. It wasn't until she grew older that she recognized the incredible disparities between her way of life and the lives of the wealthy.

She was shocked to see that Jonivan had moved into her bedroom. Dominique was in there with him, trying to get him to go to sleep. Ellie supposed it was only right. He was almost three and couldn't sleep with his mother forever. If Ellie wasn't using her room, why shouldn't he?

Yet, it saddened her to know she no longer had a place to call home.

"Hold me, Mama," Jonivan said, sitting up in his—Ellie's—bed.

"You need to go to sleep," Dominique said. "No more stalling."

Dominique's hair had grown long since Ellie had last seen her. She wore it in a French braid that reached the middle of her back.

Jonivan began to cry. "Hold me."

"You're a big boy, now, Jonivan. You don't need your mama to hold you. Now, go to sleep." Dominique leaned over and kissed his cheek.

Ellie was alarmed when Dominique said, "You're burning up! Why didn't you tell me that you don't feel well?"

"Hold me, Mama!"

Dominique picked him up and carried him to the kitchen, where Ellie's mother was washing their supper dishes.

"Mama, feel Jonivan," Dominique said.

Ellie's mother dried her hands on a dish towel and placed one on the little boy's forehead. She was wearing a new wig that curled up on the ends.

"Oh, lawd. Let me find the thermometer."

Poor Jonivan, Ellie prayed to Deimos. *No wonder he wanted to be held. He doesn't feel well. Can we go inside?*

Deimos took her hand and helped her through the walls and into the kitchen, where Dominique sat at the table holding Jonivan, who had a thermometer in his mouth. Ellie's mother dried and put away the dishes.

"Has it been three minutes yet?" Dominique asked.

"Go ahead and check it."

Dominique took the thermometer from Jonivan's mouth. "One hundred and four!"

"He needs to be seen," Ellie's mother said. "I'll take him to the emergency room."

"You're tired, Mama."

"You have to work tomorrow, and that's more important. I'll sleep tomorrow while he naps."

"No. I'll go. I can make it through one day without sleep."

Ellie sighed. Her family never seemed to catch a break. There was always something.

Is there anything we can do to help? she asked Deimos.

We can aske Hypnos to keep away from Dominique tomorrow, but that's about it. It's too risky to pray to Apollo.

At least it's something.

Let's go make a plan for how we're going to get a message to Phobos and Cupid.

Can you put a post card in the mailbox letting my mother and sister know I'm okay?

Good idea.

They flew to the front of the house, where Deimos conjured a post-card from Italy—postmarked and signed from Ellie, with a note saying she'd visit as soon as she could.

After she put the card in the mailbox, Ellie wished she could hug her mother and sister and Jonivan. Instead, she wiped her tears and flew away with Deimos, back to Selene's cave on Mont Forel.

CHAPTER THREE

A Risky Meeting

When Deimos and Ellie returned to Selene's cave, they found Hermes waiting for them.

Deimos feared something must be wrong for the god to have returned so soon after his last visit.

"Has something happened?" Deimos asked.

Hermes flinched. Deimos had forgotten that he and Ellie weren't visible to him.

"I see you're already putting the helm to use," Hermes said as Ellie removed it from her head.

"What's happened?" Deimos asked again.

"Have you been to Phobos?" Hermes asked.

"We were practicing," Ellie said.

"That's too bad," Hermes said. "Because I need the helm."

"What?" Ellie and Deimos said together.

"Why?" Deimos asked.

"Hades has set up a meeting with Athena," Hermes said. "I need the helm for Hephaestus. Athena doesn't know he's a rebel."

"Why does he need to attend?" Deimos asked. "Phobos must be mad with worry. I know I would be."

"We want Thanatos to share the protection of the helm with Hephaestus," Hermes explained. "He's a suspected, but not a known, rebel. And we want him there for his power of disintegration, just in case Athena has a trick up her sleeve."

"Disintegration?" Ellie repeated. "What's that?"

"The ability to multiply himself, like Hip," Deimos said.

"Hip?" Ellie asked.

"Hypnos," Hermes clarified.

"Can we fly over to the ranch real quick first?" Ellie pleaded. "We'll come right back with the helm."

"The meeting is already in progress," Hermes said. "I need it now. The rebels may be in danger."

Deimos took the helm and handed it over to Hermes. "Should I come with you?"

"Absolutely not," Hermes said. "Stay here and watch over Hecate."

"Selene's here," Deimos pointed out. "And Ellie—who's been a fast learner. If the loyalists attack, you'll need all the help you can get."

"Be careful not to make Athena panic," Hermes said. "And remain with the helm at all times."

"Will do," Deimos said.

"Shall we go then?" Hermes offered an elbow to Deimos.

Deimos linked arms with Hermes as the messenger god put on the helm.

"Stay put," Deimos said to Ellie before the fastest god alive swept him into the sky.

They hadn't been flying for long when Hermes pointed to a castle in Scotland, where Hephaestus waited in his chariot on the highest turret.

Left alone with the sleeping gods in Selene's cave, Ellie didn't know what to do with herself. She was worried that Hermes wouldn't be able to loan her the helm a second time and her chance of getting a message to Phobos had been lost. She glanced at the chariot parked near the mouth of the cave. Would anyone notice if she bridled the horses and flew across the sky toward Texas? Wouldn't they assume she was the moon goddess?

But how would she get word to Phobos? If only she could drop a note to him somehow. Maybe she could write a note on a rock and throw it down as she passed over the ranch. She was a goddess now; surely her accuracy as a pitcher was improved.

Shouldn't she wait for Deimos to return? It would be stupid to take such a risk. But she wasn't the kind of girl who waited around for someone else to help her. Taking the chariot now, while Selene slept during the new moon, might be her only chance.

She returned her sword and shield to the couch and searched the cave for a loose rock. She came across pebbles that were too small and larger rocks that could kill if they landed on a person or animal. She needed one the size of a golf ball—though even a rock of that size could injure someone. She'd have to be careful.

Once she'd found the right rock, she then needed something to write with. Doubting Selene had a black Sharpie in the cave, she wondered if she had the power to conjure anything. She could conjure the weapons that had been given to her, but what about other things? The boys had been able to dress her. Could she do that, too?

Ellie sat at the wooden table with the rock in her hand and closed her eyes, trying to focus.

Her mind wandered to the night she wore the emerald-green dress with the low back in Cupid and Psyche's castle—her first night alone with Phobos. He had made her laugh by saying, "Are you a beaver? Because, dam!"

Before she realized she'd lost focus, the emerald gown appeared on her. She looked down at her lap and felt the satin fabric with disbelief.

"Well, that answers that question," she murmured.

She regained focus and dressed herself in jeans and her favorite long-sleeved lavender top and flat-heeled ankle boots. Then she imagined the black Sharpie her mother kept in the kitchen drawer.

Nothing happened.

"Well, damn."

Maybe she could scratch her message into the rock. She was a goddess with super strength, but could her fingernail hold up?

On the rock, she carved an "I."

"It works!" she said to herself.

Then she carved: *I'm safe--E*

Thinking Phobos would be worried about his brother, too, she wrote on the other side: *D is 2.*

She focused again and made a pair of her white socks appear, having the idea of putting the rock in the socks to make it more noticeable and less likely to hurt someone.

Now, she needed to bridle Crescent and Luna without waking Hecate or Selene.

Deimos remained with Hermes, Hephaestus, and Thanatos in Hephaestus's chariot near the mouth of a cave beneath the acropolis in Athens. Athena had insisted on meeting Hades there, where she kept her pet, Amphisbaena—a serpent dragon with a head on both ends. Each head was made of shiny blue scales and was crowned with bright red spikes down the center. Intense black eyes peered from two slits above a short snout and a darting, forked tongue.

Persephone and Hypnos had remained behind with the Furies to protect the Underworld, in case the meeting was a ruse on Athena's part, to lure the rebels away from the Underworld to make it vulnerable to attack.

It was high noon on this side of the world, and the acropolis was crawling with tourists, despite the cold. Deimos hated being on the outskirts of the action taking place inside the cave—though he'd rather be on the outskirts than not there at all. At least he could see and hear what was happening, even if he couldn't participate.

"Show me the helm," Athena was saying from where she stood beside her serpent dragon.

Deimos felt a bead of sweat form on his forehead.

"I have no intention of capturing you," Hades said. "You're free to go whenever you please. I only want to tell you my side of things."

"I've heard your side, haven't I?"

"Perhaps," Hades said. "But I get the feeling you haven't been listening—none of you have—or we wouldn't be at odds with one another."

Athena frowned. "If you're trying to get into my good graces, I'm afraid it's not working."

"I don't care about your good graces," Hades said. "We both know that ship sailed centuries ago. I want what's best for the Olympians."

"Speak your mind, and make it quick," she said, "before I'm missed."

"What would be the purpose of the Fates to put us through a reckoning, do you think?" Hades asked.

"To test us," she said.

"Precisely. And by what criteria do you suppose the Fates would judge us?"

"That's the mystery, isn't it?" Athena challenged.

"Not if you think about it," Hades said. "Let's consider what we know of the Fates. Shall we?"

"If you make it snappy."

"They spin, measure, and cut the threads of mortal life," Hades said. "They enforce rules on the gods that make it impossible for us to alter human destiny. While they allow the gods to help a person to switch destinies with another, they only allow it when both mortals agree."

"So?" Athena asked. "What's your point?"

"The Fates also require that only the strongest among us has the power of apotheosis—the ability to transform a mortal into a god."

"I know what apotheosis is."

"And the strongest god among us gets his power by a combination of birth—something decided by the Fates—and the prayers and support of mortals."

"Do you have a point?" Athena asked.

"The only gifts the Fates have ever given to the gods are three—the helm, the trident, and the lightning bolt. Do you know why I and my brothers were given these gifts?"

"To help balance out the power among the gods, so no one god would become all powerful."

"Exactly," Hades said. "And who benefits the most from that balance?"

Athena crossed her arms and cocked her head to one side. "I was going to say the Olympians, but those who *most* benefit are mortals."

"Yes!" Hades said, clapping his hands together, causing Amphisbaena to glower down at him. "Sorry, Amphisbaena. Did I startle you?"

"Your point seems to be that everything the Fates do is for the protection of mortals."

"Yes. Zeus may have come up with the idea to *create* mortals, but the Fates have made it their mission to impose checks and balances to ensure their survival as a species. So, given that the Fates value the survival of humans, do you, oh wise and beautiful Athena, believe that we could possibly pass their test by killing one of them?"

"She's no longer mortal," Athena said. "You saw to that."

"As a form of protection."

Athena stroked Amphisbaena's back. "You've given me a lot to think about, Lord Hades."

"But I haven't persuaded you?"

"Not yet. You see, there's still the matter of Apollo's visions, with Mount Olympus crumbling and all that."

"And from whom does Apollo receive his visions?" Hades asked.

"The Fates."

"Precisely."

"You seem quite confident, Lord Hades."

"And you are not, gray-eyed Athena. Why is that?"

"I'm loyal to my father."

"He swallowed your mother while you were still in her womb, to save his own power. Why are you loyal to him?"

"That's rich, coming from a father who once tried to kill his child while it was still forming in Persephone's womb."

"What I did or did not do has no bearing on the decision that's to be made today," Hades said. "The Fates have designed a test, and we will not pass it if we destroy the girl or her innocent babes."

"I'll give you my answer in two days," Athena said just before she flew away.

Amphisbaena hissed at Hades, who flew to the chariot and took the helm.

"What are *you* doing here?" Hades said to Deimos. "You had *one job*: to protect Hecate and Ellie. Hermes, you should have known better."

"It's the new moon," Hermes said. "Selene's there."

"She'll be sleeping," the lord of darkness said. "Hurry back."

"But, Lord Hades," Deimos said. "I thought I could use your helm to get a message to my brothers."

"Not today. I intend to follow Athena to Mount Olympus to hear their deliberations."

"How do you know they'll deliberate?" Hermes asked.

"I know Athena," the lord of the Underworld replied. "She'll try to reason with her father before ever considering a betrayal."

"When do you suppose I might have it?" Deimos asked. "The helm, that is."

"I can't make you any promises."

Hades whistled, and, within seconds, his chariot appeared. He soon disappeared into the bright sky.

Hephaestus pulled a lever and pressed a button before his chariot took off.

"Sit low and out of sight," he said to Deimos.

Ellie struggled to maintain control of the reins as Crescent and Luna flew through the crisp air to the west. The horses seemed to fly of their own accord, without any guidance from Ellie. She supposed they believed they were traveling their usual route around the world.

How would she get them to fly low over Texas, close enough for her to pitch the rock into the old shack on the Garcia ranch?

Using the reins did no good, and she was afraid that, if she shouted out commands, she'd be overheard and captured by loyalists. Then, it dawned on her: she could speak to them telepathically.

Dear Crescent and Luna, I know this isn't your usual thing, but I need your help. Wouldn't it be nice to do something different for a change? Here's what I need: When we are directly over Texas, I need you to race down to the treetops, help me to find the Garcia ranch near Del Río, and hold us there long enough for me to pitch this rock through Phobos's window.

To her surprise, the horses agreed. However, now that she was in the chariot and carrying out the plan, she realized how stupid it was. How ironic would it be if, in trying to let Phobos know she was safe, she was captured?

I'm a goddess, she said to herself. *I can do this.*

Deimos regretted not using the helm to get a message to Phobos when he'd had the chance. He'd justified taking Ellie to see the northern lights by calling it practice, when, really, he'd wanted to impress her.

The prayers from Phobos had become almost morbid: *If you're not swallowed or imprisoned, take care of her. She belongs with you.*

Deimos shifted on his knees in the bottom of Hephaestus's chariot and prayed to Athena for wisdom.

Where are you? Athena asked telepathically.

You know I can't tell you that, he replied.

"What in Hades?" Hermes cried from where he sat beside Hephaestus.

Deimos looked up to see Selene's chariot flying west without a driv-er.

C H A P T E R   F O U R

Abduction

Ellie glared at Ares as he pushed her against the wall of the deep, dark cave. His red hair was as vibrant as his sons', but his blue eyes were cold, and his mouth was a grim straight line.

His forearm pressed against her throat. "Not too bright, are you?"

"Where am I?" Her wrists had been shackled with adamantine handcuffs. They didn't prevent her from flying or running, but they made it impossible for her to god-travel or to conjure her sword and shield. She tried to break them apart, to wriggle her wrists free, to bash them against her hip as Ares pinned her against the wall, but they wouldn't budge.

"Wouldn't you like to know?" He glanced down at her mouth. "I'm curious to learn why my sons are so dazzled by you, even as they carry the arrows of hate."

Nausea swept through her belly. She sucked in her lips and clenched her fists.

"You seem repulsed by the idea," Ares said with a wry grin. "I'm surprised. I thought you liked being shared."

If she weren't so afraid, she'd spit in his face.

"Choose one of my sons, and I'll release you," he said.

Her eyes widened with surprise. "You'll let me go?"

"If you *choose*."

She took a deep breath and told herself that it didn't matter what she said to him; she just needed to pick one to be free. But what if Ares used this against his sons, to hurt them? She needed to be careful about what she said. Phobos was without powers and already in a morbidly dark place. Deimos, on the other hand, could hear her prayers and explanations, if Ares were to taunt him.

"Phobos," she said. "I choose Phobos."

Ares lifted his brows. "I would have lost, had I wagered. Deimos is more responsible and would make a better father."

She found his words ironic, considering what a terrible father Ares was, but she held her tongue, wanting only to be free.

"Well?" she said. "Can I go now?"

He pressed his mouth hard against hers, suckling her lips, plunging his tongue against hers. She was tempted to bite it but was afraid he'd find pleasure in it.

Stepping back and releasing her, he said, "I just don't see it."

She took off running. She had no idea which way to go, but she had to get away from that foul god as soon as possible. She could hear his laughter in the distance, and, once she realized he wasn't following, she slowed her pace and studied the walls of the cave, looking for light.

Deimos leapt into Selene's chariot and took the reins. "Time to go home, girls!"

Hephaestus and Hermes followed in Hephaestus's chariot as Deimos directed Luna and Crescent back to their mistress's abode. He knelt in the chariot, to be as inconspicuous as possible.

Selene was waiting just inside her cave, her long, luminous hair and equally luminous robe blown back with the wind, her silver eyes glaring at him.

"Out!" She pointed her finger toward the frosty sky. "You and your girlfriend are no longer welcome. Never in my very long lifetime has anyone taken my chariot without my permission! That ungrateful—where is she?"

Deimos climbed to his feet. "Ellie? She isn't *here*?"

The moon goddess raised her fists and shouted, "She stole my chariot!"

The entire mountain shook.

Deimos turned to Hermes. "Oh, my god. She must have gone to Phobos."

"Get out!" Selene screeched again.

Deimos flew from the mouth of the cave and hovered near Hephaestus's chariot. His chest tightened, and his throat felt as if it were closing. Ellie had gone to Phobos. Had he been wrong in thinking she loved them equally? Was Phobos her choice?

"We need to get out of here," Hermes warned. "If loyalists spotted Selene's chariot gone rogue, they're on their way. Deimos, get in."

As Deimos flew toward Hephaestus's chariot, arrows came at them, and one struck Deimos in the back. Hephaestus flew his chariot into the safety of Selene's warded cave, but Deimos was stung by something that pulsed through him, causing him to fall through the air, helpless.

Before he hit the side of the mountain, a pair of arms caught him.

"Father?" Deimos said, dazed. Was his father helping him?

Ares slapped a pair of adamantine cuffs onto Deimos's wrists. "I asked Ellie to choose. Guess who she picked?"

Deimos stared up at his father blankly as they continued to fly through the air. "Where are we going?"

"She chose Phobos. Just thought you should know."

"What are you doing?" Deimos asked, closing his eyes to keep his head from spinning.

"Saving us—all of us. If you'd only listen to your mother and me, we wouldn't be in this mess."

When Deimos opened his eyes, he found himself lying in a dark cave near a thin stream.

"Are you hungry?" Ares asked him.

"Where am I?"

"Safe. You were struck by Poseidon's trident, but you'll heal. Stay put until all of this is over."

Before Deimos could ask more, his father disappeared.

Ellie had been running through the cavern tunnels for what seemed like hours without any end in sight. There'd been forks along the way, and she'd chosen her path randomly. A few times, she'd doubled back to choose a different path. Frustrated and tired, she slumped on a rock to think. She was about to pray to Deimos when she sensed something coming toward her from around the bend.

She froze and listened. Heavy footfalls. She sniffed. An animal. She tried to look with her goddess vision through the rock but failed. Again.

The labyrinthine cave was enchanted. It was the only explanation she could think of for her inability to see through its walls.

Not wanting to be heard, she lifted from the ground, to fly, but hit her head on the top of the cave. The pain wasn't as sharp as she would have expected, but it still hurt and surprised her. She cried out and dropped to her feet.

The beast stopped in its tracks. She heard him sniffing, assessing.

She took off running in the opposite direction. The cave turned and twisted, narrowed and widened, but she kept running.

When she came to a fork, she paused. Both tunnels were dark. Through which had she already passed? The one on the right sounded as though it had running water. She hadn't come across water yet. And maybe the water would lead her out of the cave.

She heard the beast gaining on her, so she ran to the right, hoping she would soon see light.

Despite hours of frustration, she was an optimist. There had to be an end to this dreary maze soon.

The creature behind her snorted. She turned back to see a terrifying bull coming toward her. His head was huge, with horns that curved from each side to a sharp point. His mouth was pulled back, exposing sharp teeth. She had a flashback of Rusty the bull at the Garcia ranch. Yet, this wasn't a regular bull—he ran on his hind legs. When she glanced back a second time, she noticed his legs, arms, chest—everything except his head was that of a man.

"Who are you? And why are you here?" he demanded as he neared her.

She kept running, following the water whenever she came to a fork. She glanced back again, to find the monster gaining on her. She turned back and ran smack into…Deimos?

"Deimos? Oh my god, is that really you?" she asked, noticing that he, too, was wearing adamantine handcuffs.

Before he could answer, she glanced back at the monster and said, "Run!"

Deimos grabbed her by the arm. "We can't outrun him. I don't think he'll hurt us."

The minotaur caught up to them, panting. "Deimos? What's going on?"

"Asterion, meet Ellie. Ellie, meet Asterion."

"Huh?" Ellie, trembling, gasped for air.

"Why are you here?" the minotaur asked.

"My father. He's imprisoned us here. I've just been hit by the trident."

Ellie looked at him in horror. "Are you okay?"

"Getting there," Deimos said.

"Why would your father do this to you?" Asterion asked.

"It's kind of a long story," Deimos said. "But the gist of it is that Ellie has been seen in visions by several seers with the pillars of Mount Olympus crumbling, so now a bunch of gods are afraid of her and her unborn twins. My dad's one of them. So is my mom."

"That's awful," the minotaur said. "Why don't you come to my chambers, and have a rest, and then I'll help you out of here?"

"Really?" Ellie's brows lifted. "You'll help us?"

"Why wouldn't I?" the minotaur seemed offended.

"Because, because I think I've heard of you," Ellie said. "Aren't you the minotaur?"

"I prefer Asterion."

"Is it true that you eat people who get lost in your labyrinth?"

"Only when there's nothing else to eat."

Ellie gaped.

"Just kidding," Asterion said. "I'm a vegetarian. I eat mostly grains, but I have a reputation to keep, so don't tell anyone. Come on, follow me."

As they followed the minotaur through the winding tunnels, Deimos explained to Ellie, "The stories you've heard are based on *some* truth. You see, Asterion's labyrinth was created long ago by a guy called Daedalus, back when the gods wanted to imprison Asterion."

"Why did they want to do that?" Ellie asked.

"I thought I already told you this story," Deimos said.

"You've told me too many to remember."

Deimos laughed. "Okay. Poseidon sent King Minos, who ruled Crete at the time—that's where we are, the island of Crete—a snow-white bull to be sacrificed to Poseidon."

"Why would Poseidon want the bull to be sacrificed to him?" Ellie asked as they continued to follow Asterion through the maze.

"It's a pride thing," Asterion said. "The gods like to keep powerful people in their place by testing them."

"Oh," Ellie said.

"Well, King Minos decided to keep the beautiful white bull and sacrificed another," Deimos said.

"Which angered Poseidon," the minotaur added.

"Right," Deimos said. "To punish Minos, Poseidon had Daedalus create a device that would enable Minos's wife, Pasiphae, to have sex with the snow-white bull."

"Why would she do such a thing?" Ellie asked.

"Poseidon forced Cupid to make her fall in love with the bull," Deimos said. "Poseidon had leverage over my brother. I can't now recall what."

"Anyway," the minotaur said. "I was the result—and really, the only one who suffered from what Minos did. It sucks."

"Oh," Ellie said again.

"They didn't know what to expect from me," Asterion said. "And probably because I was unloved for most of my life, I was beastly for a long time. I like the reputation, though, because it keeps people away—except for the thrill seekers. For their own safety, I do my best to frighten them away, so they don't die of starvation trying to find their way out again. I used to eat them, but not anymore."

"What changed?" Ellie asked.

"I guess I developed a more sophisticated palate," he said. Then he added, "Just kidding. My half-sister, Ariadne, took pity on me a few hundred years ago. She lives with me here, most of the time. She's taught me how to care. I think the instinct to care was there all along, but fear suppressed it. You know what I mean?"

"Yes," Ellie said. "I do. It happens in impoverished areas among mortals. Kids are born to parents who are strung out on drugs because they've been beat down by structural violence and oppression, and the kids are left to their own devices. Some turn out fine. Others go wild, just trying to survive."

Deimos squeezed her hand.

"That's how it was for my mother," Ellie added. "She had to raise herself. *Her* mother was always depressed. Her father left when she was a baby. She had to find her own way from a very young age, and she didn't have a sister, like you, to help her."

"You sound like you miss her," Asterion said.

Ellie brushed a tear from her cheek. "I guess I do."

The tunnel led to a larger cave. It had the height of Selene's cave, along with the stalactites. But it lacked the luminous glow.

There was a bit of light coming from a hearth, surrounded by chairs and a low table.

"Have a seat," Asterion said. "I'll get you something to drink."

Deimos led Ellie to the grouping of chairs by the fire. He'd never been to Asterion's private chambers. The few times he'd interacted with the minotaur had taken place near the mouth of the labyrinth or on Mount Olympus.

Asterion handed them each a golden goblet. "Wine from Dionysus. It's the best."

"Is it safe for the babies?" Ellie asked.

"A little wine won't hurt," Deimos said.

Ellie put the goblet to her lips.

The minotaur frowned. Then, just as Ellie was about to drink, he swatted her goblet to the floor, where it cracked in half.

"What the devil?" Deimos asked.

CHAPTER FIVE

The Labyrinth

Ellie stared up at the minotaur, speechless. Every fiber in her being had told her to run from him, and this behavior only solidified her instinctual fear.

"I'm sorry," he said. "I can't believe I almost went through with it."

"Went through with what?" Deimos asked.

"I wasn't honest with you before," he said. "I knew Ares brought you here, and I knew why."

Deimos moved to Ellie's side and stood between her and the minotaur. "What's going on?"

"Ares has Ariadne—my sister," Asterion said. "He said he'd return her if I put an herb in Ellie's wine."

"What herb?" Ellie asked. "Why?"

"I don't know the name of it. It was supposed to cause...to cause you to miscarry." Asterion covered his bull eyes with his human hands. "I'm so sorry. Ares said he'd swallow my sister."

"Thank god you saw the light," Deimos murmured. "Did Ares say how long you have before he carries out his threat?"

"He said the herb would take about a week. I was supposed to summon him at the first sign of blood. He's got the entrance heavily guarded. You wouldn't have been able to leave."

Ellie clutched her belly and burst into tears. "How can I possibly protect my babies from so many powerful, evil gods?"

"They aren't evil," Deimos said.

"How can you defend them?" Ellie glared up at him.

Deimos touched her shoulder. "I've seen what fear can do to people—and to gods."

Ellie shook her head. "How can they even feel fear, with Phobos stripped of his powers?"

"It's *because* his powers are gone that they feel fear," Deimos explained. "They feel it more intensely than when Phobos had his powers."

"I don't understand," Ellie said.

"Think of the pantheon like you would the human body. When a human loses an appendix or a gall bladder, the rest of the body compensates. That's what happens when one of us loses our powers. Fear didn't just go away. It became spread out over all the gods in the pantheon—including you. But, because none of us is the god of fear, it affects us differently than it does Phobos. It makes us feel fear, even while we instigate the feeling in others. It's compounding the fear. Does that make sense?"

Ellie sighed. "A little. Deimos, I just want to protect my babies. What do I do?"

"I can't let Ares swallow my sister," Asterion said.

"No," Deimos agreed. "We need a plan."

"Is there someplace where I can lie down?" Ellie asked. "I'm exhausted."

"You can stay in Ariadne's room," the minotaur replied. "I'll show you where it is. Follow me."

Ellie followed, with Deimos taking up the rear. They left the main chamber and passed through a winding tunnel. The minotaur stopped before a wooden door and opened it.

The room was lovely. The walls possessed a luminous lavender glow that both soothed and uplifted Ellie's mood. A big bed, set up high on an iron frame with a thick white comforter, took up most of the space. Water ran along the farthest wall and pooled into a large basin, the size of a hot tub, where there were bottles of what appeared to be soaps, shampoos, and lotions along the ledge. Above the basin hung a round gilded mirror. On the opposite wall from the pool was a small table with a single chair and a mug half-filled with liquid—possibly tea. Across from the bed was an empty hearth and, above it, a mantle with framed photos, decorative boxes, and two paintings—one of Asterion and another of a god Ellie had not yet met.

It was a striking god with gold hair worn in two French braids. Bold, green eyes glared from the canvas, and a bare tan chest was ripped and magnificent.

"Would you like a fire?" Asterion asked.

"Please," Ellie said.

A fire burst forth from the pit of the hearth and immediately added a cozy atmosphere to the already lovely room.

"Thank you, Asterion," Deimos said. "I'll stay with Ellie for a while. I promise to be thinking of a way to save Ariadne."

"I can't lose her," he said. "She's my only family. My only friend."

"We'll think of something," Deimos said. "I promise."

Deimos closed the door of Ariadne's room after Asterion had left. Ellie climbed onto the big bed and slipped beneath the white comforter.

"This bed is almost as comfortable as the one I slept in at Cupid's castle," she said. "Thank goodness for small pleasures. Deimos, what are we going to do?"

He crawled beneath the covers beside her. Because of their adamantine cuffs, it was difficult for him to hold her. He lay on his side, facing her, bent his arms at the elbows, and cupped her face. "Right now, I'm thankful that we're together. I can't imagine how things might have gone down had my father not brought me here, too."

A tear slipped down her cheek. "I don't even want to think about it."

Deimos sighed. "Get some rest, Ellie. Sleep if you can. I may try to sleep, too. I can't remember the last time I did—it's been that long."

She kissed him and said, "I love you, Deimos." Then she said, "By the way, your father tricked me into making a choice between you and Phobos. Since he didn't make me swear an oath on that river—what's it called?"

"The Styx."

"That's right. Since he didn't make me swear, and since I knew I could pray to you with explanations, I said Phobos. But I didn't mean it. I don't know if he said anything to you…"

"No, he didn't," Deimos lied, feeling ashamed that he'd ever doubted her love.

"Good. Because I still have no idea what I'm going to do. The only thing I can think to do is to let the Fates decide when we learn which of you is the father. But even then—honestly, Deimos, I just love you both so much."

"Maybe you don't have to choose," he said.

She lifted her brows. "What?"

"Maybe you don't have to choose. I think I've come to terms with the fact that you love us equally. And I love my brother, too. I couldn't stand to see him hurt if you chose me. I don't know how we'd carry on. We have to work every day together. It would be impossible. And I'm confident enough in my love for you to know I could share you with him."

Ellie's mouth fell open. He leaned in and caressed her open lips with his. She returned his kiss, licking him and sending shocks of pleasure to every muscle in his body.

Then she stopped. "Deimos, what if Phobos doesn't feel the same way?"

"He won't, at first. But maybe we can talk him into it."

Ellie smiled at him. She had that look in her eyes that said she wanted him.

"I find I'm not quite as sleepy as I was," she said. "What about you?"

"I think I can go without a while longer," he whispered with a grin. "Is there something else you'd rather do?"

"Hmm. Let me think."

"I've got ideas." He playfully bit her bottom lip.

"Oh, Deimos. You hurt me so good."

Ellie was awakened sometime later by what she, at first, thought was Deimos's voice, but when she sought his face, she found him sound asleep beside her. Then she realized Phobos was praying to her again.

I found your message, Ellie. Thank you. I feel better knowing that you're safe. And I suppose I'm not sad about Deimos being safe, too.

That was a joke. I'm glad you're both safe. And as I've said before, I want you to be happy. The more I think about it, the more I feel you're better off with him— though it kills me to say it. I love you, Ellie, and always will.

I hope you can hear me. It's night in Texas, and I'm exhausted from a hard day's work. The Garcias had us work extra hard today because they're taking off tomorrow afternoon after church to celebrate their Christmas. There is so much more work to this calving thing than I ever realized.

And Psyche is pretty useless, by the way. Unlike you, she can't stand to get her hands dirty. She was a princess, you see, and then she went from being a princess to a goddess. She's never had to do manual labor. She mopes and complains all friggin' day.

But I do have one good thing to report. Remember Deimos the cat? A few nights ago, he was accidentally left outside of the main house. I think Jaquelyn had gone out on a date—she's dating a boy from her school. Anyway, Deimos climbed in bed with me and has been sleeping with me every night since. He reminds me of you and the good old days.

Well, I'm bushed. Good night, Ellie. I love you. And Merry Christmas, if that's something you celebrate. Deimos the cat says goodnight, too. Don't you, kitty?

Ellie smiled and whispered, "Good night, Phobos and Deimos."

Deimos yawned. "Hmm? Did you say something?"

"I didn't mean to wake you," she said. "I was laughing at Phobos."

"Do you know that he yammers in my ear all day long?"

"Really?"

"I don't blame him. We've spent our whole lives together. He's not used to being away from me. He thinks he's so damn funny, though. If you ever see me rolling my eyes, it's probably because of something my brother said in a prayer to me."

Ellie giggled. "He told me he's been sleeping with Deimos the cat. Could that be a sign that he might be okay with sharing a bed with us?"

Deimos smirked. "I doubt it. Maybe. With you in the middle at all times."

"I was thinking about that time in Circe's tree."

"I think about it often."

She nestled her check against his chest, wishing she could put her arms around him. "These darn cuffs."

"Hey, want to take a bath? It might make you feel better."

"I'd love to," she said.

As she struggled to climb from the rumpled and twisted covers, Deimos flew up effortlessly and hovered in the air.

"I keep forgetting that I can do that," she said, joining him.

He cupped her cheeks and kissed her.

"Do I have morning breath?" she asked between kisses.

"Gods don't have morning breath," he murmured against her lips.

"Should we disrobe and hop in?" She glanced down at the basin, which was about five feet in diameter.

"Slowly," he said. "I like to go slow."

Ellie grinned. She was glad that he and Phobos were different in that way. It was nice to have variety on such extreme ends of the spectrum. Phobos was fast and passionate with his love making; whereas, Deimos was slow, gentle, and seductive.

"*You* do it," she said. "Take off my clothes as fast or as slow as you'd like."

He backed up a few feet and took off her top—along with the bra. Even though she knew he could see her through her clothes, there was still something sexy and arousing about being bare breasted in front of him. She felt her nipples harden.

"My turn," she said.

"Go for it."

"You haven't taught me this yet. It's not like conjuring and replacing weapons."

"No, it isn't. And I hope you don't mind if I teach you another time, because, right now, I just want to ravish you."

"Oh, my."

Her pants and undies vanished.

He flew to her and took her hand, leading her to the basin. Then he made his own clothes disappear before climbing in beside her.

The water was cool, but the temperature didn't affect her. The feel of the water soaking her skin was soothing.

She was surprised when he took a bottle of shampoo and began to give her a bath. Then she purred when she rubbed her in all the right places.

"I guess I'll be sparkling clean there," she half-said and half moaned.

It wasn't long before she was biting her lip and crying out in ecstasy.

Ellie wasn't sure how long she and Deimos had remained together in Ariadne's room in the minotaur's labyrinth. Without access to daylight, the hours ran together. Was it two days? Three? However long it had been, she was removing her clothing for another soak in the basin, when Deimos sat up in the bed and said, "Ellie! You have a baby bump!"

She looked down. He was right. Where her belly had been relatively flat, there was now a distinct bump. She smiled at him.

"You look so adorable," he said.

He flew to her. "I feel, deep in my heart, that I'm the father. I just know it. I don't know how to describe it."

She hoped he wouldn't be disappointed. And yet, she hoped the same for Phobos. Maybe it would be better if the paternity of the twins was left a secret, especially if she and Deimos were going to convince Phobos to be polyamorous.

"How long has it been since we came here, do you think?" she asked.

"A little more than two days. Are you hungry? We should go and talk to Asterion."

"I think we should." She rinsed herself in the basin, dried on a cotton towel she found on a shelf, and put on fresh clothes. "Have you come up with any ideas for saving Ariadne?"

Deimos glanced up at the paintings on the mantle. "I have actually. One idea, anyway. Let's go."

They retraced their steps down the winding tunnel to Asterion's main chamber. He wasn't there, but the fire was still lit. They took seats across the room at the table, where Deimos conjured up some food.

"I'm hungry for pancakes," he said. "Sound good to you?"

"Can I have some berries with mine?" Asterion asked as he entered.

"Absolutely," Deimos said. "I was hoping you would join us. I've got an idea."

CHAPTER SIX

Mount Kithairon

S tay here," Deimos said to Ellie. "We'll be right back."

"I'm scared," Ellie said.

"You're safer here than out there," Asterion said.

Ellie didn't look like she believed the minotaur.

"Go lie down in Ariadne's room," Deimos said. "We'll be right back.

Deimos watched as Ellie left the main chamber. She glanced back at him, and he gave her a reassuring nod. Then he followed Asterion in the opposite direction, through the labyrinth to the entrance, where Asterion had warned him that loyalists would be watching.

From just inside the mouth of the cave, Deimos prayed to Hermes: *Ares took Ellie and me captive. We're in the minotaur's labyrinth, bound in adamantine cuffs. The entrance is guarded. Can you come with the helm and rescue us? I have a plan.*

In reply, Hermes prayed: *I'll come as soon as I can. I don't have the helm.*

Before returning to the labyrinth, Deimos studied the landscape for signs of guards. He saw Iris and Nike—two winged goddesses—lying in the grass, throwing pebbles and chatting. He imagined they'd been stationed there since Ares took him and Ellie prisoner three days ago. Their boredom would make it that much easier for Hermes to slip past, beneath the protection of the helm.

When he reached Ariadne's room, Deimos found Ellie in bed, sobbing.

He flew to her side. Her back was to him, so he spooned her and stroked her hip.

"It's going to be okay, Ellie. Hermes is on his way."

"What if Dionysus won't help us?"

"He'd do anything for Ariadne. Like I said, he's her husband."

"Is that him, in the other painting?"

"Yeah."

"Why doesn't she live with him, if they're married?"

"She doesn't like his lifestyle. Remember what I told you about the maenads?"

"The women who enforce the oaths sworn on that river. What is it called again?"

"The Styx."

"That's it."

"They have drunken orgies most nights in the woods of Mount Kithairon with satyrs and other creatures of the night. Ariadne is more of a homebody and prefers the company of her brother."

"I don't blame her."

"Dionysus would do anything for her. He loves her and hates the other Olympians for banishing him from Mount Olympus."

"I remember you telling me this. Let's see. He's the son of Zeus but not by Zeus's wife, Hera."

"Exactly. Hera couldn't stand to see Dionysus, because he was a constant reminder of Zeus's betrayal."

"But aren't there other children of Zeus who don't belong to Hera? Like Hermes?"

"Yes, but unlike Dionysus, they stood up to Hera and had more support from Zeus."

"And you think we can trust Dionysus?" Ellie rolled over to face him.

"We don't have much choice."

Ellie wasn't sure how it happened, but she soon found herself standing in the throne room of Hades surrounded by a group of rebel gods.

Hypnos approached her. His dark blond hair blew in the wind as he said, "You're dreaming, Ellie. This was the only way we could find to communicate with you. I've been waiting forever for you to fall asleep. I'm so stoked it finally happened."

The adamantine cuffs were gone. Everything seemed real. She wanted to believe it *was* real. "I'm dreaming?"

"These other gods are figments," Hypnos said. "We're not in the throne room. We're in the Dreamworld. Watch."

He turned to the lord of the Underworld and said, "Figment, I command you to show yourself!"

An eel-like creature flew in circles in the air, giggling, before it flew away.

Hypnos turned to Ellie. "Understand?"

"I think so." Ellie blinked.

"Listen carefully, okay?" Hypnos said. "And repeat this message to yourself, so you're more likely to remember it when you wake up, okay?"

Ellie nodded.

"Don't trust Hermes. He's been talking to the loyalists."

"We need the helm to escape the labyrinth," she said. "I thought he was bringing it to us."

"He doesn't have the helm," Hypnos said. "I'll come for you as soon as I can. Remember: don't trust Hermes. Repeat it for me."

"Don't trust Hermes," she said.

"Say it again," Hypnos said.

"Don't trust Hermes."

"Now wake up."

Ellie blinked and looked around Ariadne's bedroom. Deimos lay beside her, facing her.

"Everything okay?" he asked.

"I think I was dreaming."

"What about?"

"I can't remember."

He kissed her and said, "I'm glad you got some rest. It's bound to be exhausting, growing two babies. Let me see that baby bump."

She rolled onto her back. He lifted her shirt and kissed her belly.

"Oh, my gosh," Ellie cried. "I felt them. I felt them move. Isn't it too soon for that?"

"Like I said, it's different for each goddess."

"Kiss them again," she said. "I think that's what made them move."

Deimos leaned over and pressed his lips to her baby bump. Ellie smiled with glee when it happened again.

"I felt it, too!" Deimos said. "I wonder if they could sense me."

"That must be it. This is the first time I've felt anything like that."

Deimos beamed at her.

If the babies weren't his, she hoped he would never know.

They were startled by a knock at the door.

"Hermes is here," Asterion said.

Deimos leapt from the bed. "Good. Come on, Ellie."

Ellie slipped on her shoes and followed Deimos down the winding tunnel toward the main chamber, where Hermes was waiting.

"I couldn't get the helm," Hermes said.

"How did you make it past the guards?" Deimos asked.

"My speed."

"I'm not sure if it would be safe to fly us out without the helm, even with your speed," Deimos said.

"Hades is using it," Hermes explained. "Maybe I can get it later today. Meanwhile, why don't you tell me your plan?"

They sat around the table with Asterion, where snacks and goblets of wine appeared. Ellie felt uneasy. She'd been drinking from goblets in the few days she'd been there, but something felt off.

"So, what's your plan?" Hermes asked.

"Ares has Ariadne," the minotaur said.

Hermes mouth fell open. "I didn't know that."

"How could you?" Deimos asked. "Ares tried to force Asterion to poison the babies, to make Ellie miscarry."

Hermes climbed to his feet and began to pace. "Are you sure about this?"

"Yes," the minotaur said. "I was to give her an herb."

Hermes ran his hand through his dark curly hair. "They were going to kill the sweet, innocent babes?"

"Why are you so surprised?" Deimos asked.

Hermes returned to the table. "Never mind. What's the plan?"

"We want you to take us to Mount Kithairon," Deimos said, "where we can ask Dionysus for help."

"Do you know where Ariadne is being held?" Hermes asked.

"No," the minotaur said.

"Maybe Hecate can do a location spell," Deimos said. "If she's well enough."

"I doubt she is," Hermes said. "But I'll see what I can find out. Some of the loyalists still trust me. I'll go make some inquiries and be back with the helm as soon as I can."

"Great," Deimos said.

"But tell me," Hermes said. "What's your plan, beyond finding Ariadne?"

"We hope to get Dionysus and the maenads on our side," Asterion said.

"They can guard Ellie," Deimos said. "At least, until the twins are born."

Ellie felt as though something were seriously wrong, but she couldn't pinpoint what.

"Sound idea," Hermes said. "I'll be back as soon as I can."

Hermes vanished.

No sooner had Hermes vanished than Hypnos appeared, holding the helm of invisibility.

"Hypnos?" Asterion climbed to his feet. "What are you doing here?"

"I've come to help."

Ellie suddenly remembered the dream. "Don't trust Hermes."

"What?" Deimos asked.

"I tried to tell her in a dream," Hypnos explained. "Hermes is playing both sides. We aren't sure where his loyalties lie."

"Oh, no," Asterion groaned.

"I'm so sorry," Ellie said. "I couldn't remember, until just now."

"I can't believe this," Deimos said.

"Hermes seemed genuinely surprised about Ares taking Ariadne," Hip said. "And he also seemed agitated about Ares's plan to kill the babies."

"But we can't be sure," Deimos murmured. "Our plan is shot to hell."

"Not if we act fast," Hypnos said. "Let's go to Dionysus now, under the protection of the helm. If we see Hermes there, we'll come back. If not, we'll go forward with your plan."

"Ellie should stay here," Deimos said.

"But I'm going," Asterion said. "And she's not safe here alone."

"There's no time to argue," Hypnos said. "Let's go."

Ellie rubbed her abdomen. "Gods, help us."

The woods of Mount Kithairon always made Deimos shudder. He had bad memories of the time he and Phobos had participated in one of Dionysus's orgies. It had been fatal, and Deimos had come close to losing an arm forever.

He and Phobos had been young and had been learning the ways of the gods. They hadn't known that, although they could heal their wounds and regenerate their organs, they couldn't reproduce entire limbs. The body had to be preserved once the soul went to Tartarus; if it wasn't, the soul must either be placed into another body or live as a ghost forever.

It was Phobos who'd saved him. Deimos had been dancing between two half-naked maenads. He'd been drunk for the first time, enjoying the sensation of having no cares, no worries. He'd previously read a book on dance and was experimenting with different moves. He'd also read about mating rituals of different animals and had the impression that one of the maenads was coming on to him.

He'd made the mistake of grabbing her from behind and grinding against her. He'd been about to enter her when another maenad ripped his arm from his body.

Horrified as blood spurt from his shoulder, he'd become a free-for-all. A swarm of half-naked maenads would have feasted on him after his soul left his body had Phobos not managed to fight them off and collect his body and limbs.

Linked at the elbows—save Deimos and Ellie, who held hands because of the cuffs—the four gods made their way up the snow-covered mountain, through the woods, toward the clearing, where the tribe of the wine god lived. At least two dozen maenads and ten satyrs lay sleeping on beds of evergreen branches around a bonfire that was close to burning out. Dionysus lay among them between two maenads. Hermes was nowhere in sight.

Since she was the primary target of the loyalists, Ellie wore the helm. When they reached the edge of the clearing, Hip and Asterion left the protection of the helm to approach Dionysus, while Deimos and Ellie remained behind.

Deimos squeezed Ellie's hand. She was trembling. Even her teeth chattered. He knew it wasn't because of the cold.

Dionysus flinched and sat up as Hypnos and Asterion stood over him. "Have you come to party? It'll be a while before dusk, and you know we don't start until then."

"Ariadne has been captured by Ares," Asterion said. "I need your help."

Dionysus jumped to his feet. The maenads beside him stirred, rolled over, and fell back to sleep.

"Where is she?" he asked.

"We don't know yet," Hip said. "But when we do know, can we count on your help?"

"Why would Ares take her captive?"

Hip and the minotaur caught Dionysus up to speed, including the bit about not knowing if Hermes could be trusted.

"I wondered why she hadn't answered me for the past few days," the god of wine said after Hip had finished his story. "She must be trapped somewhere that won't allow prayers to get through—someplace heavily warded."

Suddenly, Deimos knew where his father had taken Ariadne. It was Ares's favorite trap. He prayed to Hip and the minotaur. *I know where she is.*

CHAPTER SEVEN

A Rescue Mission

Ellie was glad to be far away from the freaky-looking women and satyrs that had been sleeping on the mountainside with the god of wine. Back in the labyrinth in the main room, gathered around the cozy fire, she sat with Hypnos, Deimos, and Asterion as Deimos explained what they needed to do to rescue Ariadne.

"Aside from this labyrinth, the Amazonian Pit is the only place underground that's not controlled by Hades," Deimos said. "It's my father's favorite place to trap his prisoners, because one of his daughters—a demigod who died centuries ago—was the original queen."

"Hippolyta," Hypnos said.

"Yes." Deimos took a sip of his wine. "The Amazons are still loyal to Ares and let him use their pit whenever he wants."

"How do we get to it?" Ellie asked.

"*We* don't," Deimos said. "It's too dangerous—especially in your condition. You're staying here."

"Alone?"

"No," Deimos said. "The moment the loyalists become aware of our attempt to rescue Ariadne, they'll know Asterion betrayed them. They're likely to swarm the labyrinth before we make it back."

"Ellie would be safer with Hades," Hip said.

"I can't let her go until you bring me Ariadne," the minotaur said.

"What?" Ellie cried.

"Come on," Deimos complained. "You can't be serious."

"There's too much at stake. Hip, let Deimos wear the helm, so you can disintegrate."

"Disintegrate?" Ellie asked.

"Multiply," Deimos explained. "Be in many places at once."

"Which I can't do beneath the helm," Hypnos added.

"Hip and I will stay and protect Ellie and the labyrinth, in case the loyalists retaliate," the minotaur said.

Ellie didn't like that plan one bit.

"I want to go with Deimos," she said.

Deimos shook his head. "It's too dangerous."

"It's dangerous here, too," she said.

"I can stay here *and* go with Deimos," Hypnos said to Ellie. "You won't be alone with the minotaur. And Deimos won't be alone on the rescue mission."

"And we'll pick up Dionysus on the way." Deimos took Ellie's hand. "Look, I know you don't trust Asterion, I don't blame you after what he nearly did. But he's just making sure he gets his sister back. He won't hurt you."

Ellie wished she could believe him.

The location of the Amazons was a secret only a handful of gods knew. It was risky, bringing Dionysus, who might later recruit Amazons into his band of maenads, but Deimos felt he had no choice. If Hermes had alerted the loyalists, a trap would be waiting, and Deimos needed all the help he could get.

Dionysus drove his chariot, which was under the protection of the helm since Deimos, as a passenger, was wearing it. Hip rode in the back. Before reaching the Amazons, Deimos would fly ahead with the helm while Dionysus waited in the clouds in the chariot with Hip.

Deimos and Phobos had served their father with Amazonian business throughout the centuries. Not all the women were heartless, but most cared little for men. Their only purpose for men was procreation. They abducted one man at a time from different regions. They traveled by boat to every continent to increase their gene pool. A few of their spies would infiltrate a society to seek out a superior, yet vulnerable, specimen. Then a strategy for his abduction would be formed and carried out. Deimos and Phobos had often been recruited to help make the subject more malleable with panic and fear.

The Amazons took their breeding seriously, because it was the only way to maintain their way of life. They were warriors, first and foremost. If a breeder produced a male, he was slaughtered. Females had their right breasts cauterized during infancy, so as not to interfere with her use of a bow. They were trained from infancy in the ways of battle and warfare.

When Deimos first saw the training camp as a young god, he recognized the sparring tactics as those his father had forced his sons to use. From a very young age, Phobos and Deimos were required to fight to the death. But their souls always came back. This wasn't true for the Amazons, who were mortal.

The location of the tribe was a secret, but the entire world knew of their existence, and when someone needed secret warriors for a sensitive job, they could hire the Amazons to carry it out. In the old days, an interested party would have to make inquiries. It could take months before a contact could be made and a secret deal struck. These days, they used something called the Internet.

As the Amazon territory came into view, so did the guards surrounding the pit, where Ariadne was likely being held.

The grate is charged with electricity, Deimos said to his companions. *I'll rip it open and grab Ariadne. If we're exposed, attack. If not, I'll meet you here.*

Ellie returned to Ariadne's room and lay down beneath the feather comforter, trying to remain calm while Hypnos and Asterion guarded the entrance. Another Hypnos stood guard just outside the room. Yet, she didn't feel safe, and she worried that the twin babies growing inside her could tell how stressed she was feeling.

"I'm sorry if I'm stressing you out, sweet babies," she said as she clutched her belly. "Everything's going to be okay."

Tears filled her eyes as she thought of her mother and sister back home. She wished they could have been a part of her pregnancy. Dominique would have given her a baby shower and would have invited all of Ellie's teammates and friends. Shaylynn would have helped to host it. They would have played those stupid baby shower games that everyone complains about but secretly enjoys.

Ellie felt homesick for the first time in years. She wished her family could be a part of her life. Would she one day get to tell them the truth—that she was a goddess? Would her daughters know their grandma and auntie and their cousin Jonivan? Or would her babies be killed by selfish gods?

Her thoughts were interrupted by a prayer from Phobos: *Only four and a half weeks left, Ellie. My powers will be restored at the end of January. As much as I've come to care for the Garcia family, that day can't come soon enough.*

The Garcias have been talking a lot about New Year resolutions, and it got me thinking. As much as I love you and can't wait to see you again, as much as I want to be a part of your babies' lives, I'm resolved to hang back and watch you and the twins from a distance. I'm stronger than my brother. I honestly don't think he'll survive if you choose me. And the more I think about it, the more I worry that you will choose me. Because, let's face it, I got the better looks and personality.

Maybe I'm worrying for nothing. Maybe you've already chosen him. If so, good. He's better for you, and I can take pain and disappointment better than he can. I've already been gearing up for it, you see.

Trust me on this. I'm always right, most of the time.

Despite how sad his prayer was making her feel, Ellie laughed at his joke—*always right most of the time.* That was just like him to try to distract her from her pain and fear with humor. Ellie wished Phobos could hear her prayers to him. If she could, she'd tell him to stop "gearing up" for pain and disappointment. She'd tell him she could never allow him to watch from a distance. The thought of it made her sick to her stomach. If he would allow it, she wouldn't choose. She'd love them both.

But, right now, the three of them together happily ever after with the twins seemed like a pipe dream.

Deimos glared at the queen of the Amazons from where he stood, still in his adamantine shackles but now chained to the wall of the pit. At least Ariadne had managed to get away. When he'd grabbed the grate and opened the trap door, the jolt of electricity gave him convulsions, and the helm fell from his head to the bottom of the pit. Ariadne had grabbed it. The guards had captured Deimos before Ariadne could help him.

He'd been given a long leash and had been pacing in the pit, alone, until just now, when the queen had arrived, lowered from the trapdoor above on a rope by her entourage.

"We've been expecting you," she said, keeping her distance.

"Thanks to Hermes, I guess," Deimos spat.

"I don't know whom to thank," the queen said. "I only know your father promised us something in exchange for our continued cooperation."

"Oh, yeah? What?"

"You—that is, until you've successfully sired a female demigod offspring with our best breeder."

Deimos's chin must have hit the floor. "You've got to be kidding me."

"Not a chance," the queen said. "Sonja? Please join us."

A beautiful Amazon with dark brown hair and dark brown eyes entered the pit from above, lowered on the same rope as her queen. Like her queen, she wore their traditional armor and carried the traditional spear.

"Deimos, it's my pleasure to introduce you to Sonja. She's currently our fastest runner and has the best accuracy with both the spear and the bow. She has produced four promising offspring for us already—not including the two boys that we aborted. Now that we have ways of detecting the gender before birth, we don't have to waste time carrying boys to term just to get rid of them."

Deimos was disgusted. "You can't expect…"

"Oh, but I do," the queen said. "You've been signed, sealed, and delivered, courtesy of your papa—one of the few males, I might add, that we trust and have dealings with."

"This can't be happening," Deimos muttered.

"Oh, but it is," the queen said. "Don't look so disappointed. Sonja will make sure you enjoy yourself immensely, won't you Sonja?"

Sonja smiled. "It would be my pleasure, my queen."

Deimos knew his prayers of desperation to his parents went unheard, but he prayed them anyway.

"Where's Deimos?" Ellie asked, when the rescue team arrived at the labyrinth with a goddess whom she assumed was Ariadne.

The goddess had pale skin and silky raven hair.

"I'm afraid he was captured by the Amazons." Hypnos crossed the main chamber of the labyrinth to stand beside her. "I'm sorry. There's was nothing we could do."

She stared at the gods with her mouth hanging open as tears flooded her eyes. "Then make a new plan. How do you intend to rescue him?"

"I intend nothing of the kind," Dionysus said. "Now that my lovely Ariadne is safe, it's time for me to go. Sayonara."

The god of wine vanished.

Ellie turned to the Minotaur, who stood with an arm around his sister's shoulders. "Asterion, please. Deimos saved your sister. Can't you help me get him back?"

"I'll do what I can," the minotaur replied.

"Ellie, you should come with me to the Underworld," Hypnos said.

"I thought it wasn't safe. Isn't that why you sent me to Selene's cave?"

"If Zeus and the loyalists were going to attack Hades, they would have done so already," Hypnos said. "Come with me, and we'll discuss with the others what to do about Deimos."

Ellie supposed she'd rather go with Hypnos than stay with the minotaur.

"Thanks for letting me stay here," she said to Asterion. She turned to Ariadne. "It was nice to meet you. I'm Ellie, by the way."

"Good luck, Ellie," Ariadne said.

"I'll show you the way out," Asterion said.

CHAPTER EIGHT

The Wait

Deimos was brought a proper bed, table, and food and told that Sonja would be ovulating in two weeks. He should rest and eat well, because he would be expected to perform every other day for five days—a total of three encounters to ensure successful fertilization.

That meant the rebels had two weeks to find a way to get him the hell out of there.

It wasn't the prospect of having sex with a beautiful woman that alarmed him; the problem was that it would hurt Ellie—though, technically, she'd been less than monogamous with him, hadn't she? Did she really have a right to be angry with him, if he slept with another?

He knew better than that. Yes, she had a right. There was no justification for agreeing to the Amazon queen's terms. He would never want Ellie to think that his offer to share her with his brother came with the condition that he, too, would be polygamous. He was devoted to her and only her. Their situation was unique. He loved his brother as much as he loved her and couldn't stand to see him crushed. He wouldn't share her with just *anyone*; he shouldn't expect Ellie to share *him* with just anyone, either.

Besides, there was also the problem of the breeder having a child—his child—which would be destroyed if a boy and taken captive and trained as an Amazon if a girl. Deimos refused to be an absentee father.

He refused to be cruel and heartless to his children. He might be cruel, at times, to the other gods, but not to his family. Not like his parents.

Ellie stood in the throne room of the Underworld between Hypnos and Thanatos. Across from them, Hades and Persephone sat on their thrones, considering what Hypnos had reported about Deimos's capture. Three exotic goddesses, who'd been introduced to Ellie as the Furies, lingered beside their mother. Artemis paced before the hearth, scowling.

"I hate to say it," Hades said, "but Deimos is safe in the pit. The Amazons won't hurt him, because they're loyal to Ares. And Ares may be on the opposite side of this conflict, but he wouldn't approve of the unnecessary torture of his son."

Ellie disagreed. Ares had already put Deimos through hell. "So, you're just going to leave him there?"

"As my husband explained, Deimos is safer there than anywhere else. Why should we risk the capture of another?"

Ellie turned to Hypnos.

"They make a good point," he said.

Ellie's eyes filled with tears. She wanted to scream.

"However," Hades began, "I may have Thanatos take the helm and try to snag the key to your cuffs from Ares. You'll be better able to protect yourself when you're free of them."

"I need to lie down," Ellie said.

"I have an idea," Hypnos said. "Come with me."

Hypnos divided himself into two. One remained with the rebels in the throne room, while the other led Ellie down the winding corridor along the river of flames.

"Where are we going?" she asked.

"I want to show you the Fields of Asphodel," he said. "It's the entrance to the Dreamworld."

They flew from the palace of Hades and Persephone. On the opposite side of the river of fire, the ferryman carried a soul on a river of water. Ellie wondered if it was the Styx. A few moments later, they came upon a vast field of white flowers with a lavender luminous glow that reminded her of the walls in Ariadne's room. It was soothing and comforting.

"Let's stop here," Hypnos said as they descended.

Ellie yawned. "It's beautiful."

"I heard you say that you were worried about stressing the babies," he said. "You could lie down here, in the asphodel, and get the best sleep of your life. It would be good for you *and* for the twins."

"That sounds amazing." She yawned again.

"I'll wake you when I have news."

"Thanks, Hypnos."

As he flew away, she made herself comfortable on the soft flowers, breathing in their sweet perfume. She hadn't been lying there for long with her eyes closed when she heard footsteps in the distance.

She sat up and looked around. Coming toward her through the asphodel was…Deimos?

She climbed to her feet and ran to him.

"You're back?" she asked as he took her into his arms. Their adamantine cuffs were gone. She couldn't recall when they'd been removed. "How?"

"It doesn't matter," Deimos said. "We're together. That's all that matters."

He took her into his arms and reminded her of how nice it was to be there. Then he reached down to feel her abdomen.

"Where's your baby bump?" he asked.

To her horror, her belly was flat.

"Oh, there it is," he said. "The light must have created an illusion."

Ellie blinked, and her bump was back. Relieved, she wrapped her arms around Deimos.

"Don't you ever leave me again," she said.

When the guard returned to take his empty tray, Deimos rubbed his eyes. He felt woozy as everything around him seemed to float in slow motion.

"What's happening?" he asked the guard. He felt like he was speaking in slow motion.

"You've been drugged," the guard replied with a smile. Her cheeks were pink. "To help get you in the mood."

"Huh?"

The guard left the pit. Sometime later—a few minutes? A few hours?—Sonja entered the pit wearing a flimsy gown. He watched her descend on the rope. She was barefoot and smelled of lavender and roses. Her dark hair smelled fresh and clean.

"Hello, Deimos," she said as she approached his bed. "Are you ready?"

"Ready?" He was confused. "Ready for what?"

"For me," she said. She removed her gown and stood before him, naked. "For this."

Ellie basked in Deimos's kisses. Then he carried her away from the Fields of Asphodel to the hallowed-out tree on Circe's Island. To her surprise, Phobos was there, lying on the feather mattress, waiting for them.

"Phobos! Oh, my gods! I'm so happy to see you!"

"Everyone is, after they've spent any amount of time around Deimos," he said with a smirk.

Deimos rolled his eyes. "That's only true of the fools who are intimidated by my superior intellect."

"Oh, stop, you two, and kiss me!"

She lay between them, filled with joy.

Deimos softly caressed her ear with his tongue while Phobos rav-ished her neck and pinched her nipple.

"Oh, my gods," she said.

Deimos blinked and glanced around, confused and unable to recall where he was or how long he'd been out. As his vision cleared, he found himself in the Amazonian Pit, lying in bed, still cuffed and chained. He'd been dreaming of Ellie, of making sweet, sweet love to Ellie. It had felt so real.

He was brought from his reverie by the creaking of the trap door above his head. The queen descended on the rope wearing a smile.

"Good morning, Deimos," she said. "I have good news. Sonja is pregnant."

Deimos blinked again. This couldn't be happening.

"Now, we will wait a few weeks, when our seer can determine if it's a boy or a girl. If it's a boy, we'll terminate the pregnancy and resume where you left off, once Sonja is ovulating again. If it's a girl, we'll set you free. Wouldn't it be wonderful if she were pregnant with twin girls, like your lover, Ellie? I understand twins run in your family, so there's a decent chance."

Deimos glared at her, willing her to leave.

"Your breakfast is on its way, Deimos: Belgian waffles—our special-ty. You deserve it."

The queen tugged on her rope and ascended from the pit.

Deimos rolled over in the bed and willed himself to sleep, so he might escape his misery for a little while.

I know you can't hear me, Hypnos, but I'll say it anyway. Please bring me sleep.

Ellie was enjoying every moment that she lay between Phobos in Dei-mos in Circe's hollowed-out tree when suddenly Hypnos appeared out-side.

He ducked his head in and said, "Ellie, it's time to wake up. I have a surprise."

"I don't understand," she said.

Hip came into the tree and said, "Figments, I command you to show yourselves!"

Phobos and Deimos disappeared, and in their place appeared two eel-like creatures who giggled before they flew away.

"What the heck?"

"You're dreaming, remember? It's time to wake up."

Ellie stretched and yawned and found herself lying in the Fields of Asphodel with the adamantine cuffs still on her wrists. "How long have I been asleep?"

"A few weeks," Hip said.

"A few *weeks*? Are you serious?"

She sat up and noticed her baby bump had nearly doubled.

"Oh, my goodness!" she cried with glee.

"I have a surprise for you," Hypnos said. "Come with me."

He helped her to her feet, since she was still half-asleep, and led her from the fields.

"Where are we going?" she asked as they flew along the river of fire.

"To the throne room. Everyone's waiting."

Ellie's smile cracked her face in half. By everyone, had he meant Deimos? Had the rebel alliance managed to rescue Deimos from the Amazons?

They flew inside, where the gods were gathered around a table. She saw the back of his ginger head and cried, "Deimos!"

He stood up and turned to her. It was Phobos. She could tell from the dull hue of his skin that he was still without his powers. He wore a beard that she found sexy as hell.

Cupid and Psyche were there, too.

"Sorry to disappoint you," Phobos said.

"Phobos?" she rushed to him and lifted her cuffed arms over his head, for an embrace. She didn't care that the other gods were watching. "I'm so happy to see you! How? When? What's happening?"

"Have a seat, Ellie," Cupid said, offering her his chair.

She hugged him, too. "I'm so glad you're safe."

Cupid blushed as he moved another chair between her and his wife and sat. Psyche glared at Ellie. She clearly hadn't forgiven Ellie for suggesting that her powers be stripped and that she be sent to the Texas ranch.

Ellie sat at the table between Phobos and Cupid at the round table. Hades and Persephone sat across from them. To the left of Phobos sat Hypnos, Thanatos, and Artemis, and one of the Furies. On the other side of Cupid and Psyche sat another Fury, Hephaestus, and Athena.

Hades picked at his beard. "Can someone catch her up to speed?"

"What about my brother?" Phobos asked.

"As I told you," Hades began, "he's safe."

"No offense, Hades," Phobos said. "But I don't trust my father to ensure my brother's well-being. Would you trust yours?"

"Careful," the blonde Fury warned.

"Can someone please tell me what's happening?" Ellie asked.

Artemis leaned her elbows on the table. "We used the helm to bring them here."

Hephaestus, who was sharpening his blade, said, "We didn't want to risk them being imprisoned by my father and the loyalists once their sentences ended."

"They wouldn't be much good to the cause as prisoners," Hades pointed out.

"What about their powers?" Ellie asked.

"They'll be automatically restored when the sentence ends," Athena said.

"Better they're *here* when that happens," Persephone added, "than in the belly of another god."

"Amen," Phobos said. "Now to the matter of rescuing my brother."

"Not going to happen," Hades said firmly. "Drop it."

Ellie sat close to Phobos and rested her cuffed hands on his thigh, trying to comfort him. She was so relieved that he was out of harm's way. At least Deimos had his powers. Tears of gratitude sprang to her eyes.

He cupped her baby bump and whispered, "You've grown since I last saw you."

She smiled up at him. "Keep your hand there, and you'll feel them move."

"You'll have plenty of time for that later," Hades said. "For now, we need to discuss our plans."

"I felt it!" Phobos whispered.

"Manners!" the blonde-haired Fury warned.

"Sorry," Phobos said. "I haven't seen Ellie in so long, and she and the babies are all I could think about."

"Not all," the other Fury said. "You haven't stopped thinking of your brother since you arrived."

"Perhaps it would interest you to hear what Zeus told Athena about the unborn twins," Hades said.

"I don't think this is the time," Persephone said.

Hades lifted a finger. "The sooner they know, the sooner they can prepare."

"What is it?" Ellie asked, rubbing her belly. "Please, tell me."

Athena drew a deep breath. "My father told me what Hera has sensed about the twins' fraternity."

Ellie glanced at Phobos. "Maybe Persephone was right."

"I want to know," Phobos said.

Athena cleared her throat. "Unlike Phobos and Deimos, who are identical twins and who came from a single egg and sperm, these babies are fraternal, like Hypnos and Thanatos. Two eggs, two sperm."

"Whose sperm?" Phobos asked.

She could sense his heart pounding in his chest. His leg bounced nervously up and down.

"One of each," Athena said.

Ellie gawked. "What? Is that possible?"

"Apparently it is," Athena said.

Rubbing her belly, Ellie let that sink in. Each baby belonged to a different father. The Fates weren't going to choose for her, after all—not that she would have allowed the paternity of the babies to decide. She was in too deep with both brothers.

Ellie turned to Phobos. "One belongs to you and the other to Deimos."

Phobos was frowning. "I was so sure they were both mine."

"Are you disappointed?" Ellie asked.

"Of course."

"I'm sorry."

"I guess it's better than being cut out of the equation altogether."

"I would never have done that."

Phobos lifted his brows. "You've made your choice?"

"We'll talk later."

"Yes," Hades said. "That's a good idea. Hephaestus, please share with the others what you told me this morning."

"The loyalists are planning to attack the Underworld," Hephaestus said. "I don't know when but soon."

"We need to move Ellie as soon as possible," Artemis said.

Persephone sprang to her feet. "I've given this a lot of thought, and I have a plan."

CHAPTER NINE

Demeter's Winter Cabin

Deimos awoke when the trapdoor above creaked open. He watched the queen of the Amazons as she was lowered into the pit on her rope.

"I have good news, Deimos. Sonja is carrying a girl. As soon as we know the fetus is out of any danger, we'll release you."

Deimos was overwhelmed with feelings. He was happy to be having a daughter but sad that he'd never know her.

He'd find a way to know her. It wasn't right.

"How long will that take?" he asked.

"Two weeks. Meanwhile, there's someone here who'd like to speak with you."

Ares flew into the pit. He was wearing his battle armor—something he only wore during conflicts with the gods. Had things gotten worse out there?

"How could you do this to me?" Deimos said angrily. "Your own son?"

"It's nothing I haven't done myself, plenty of times."

"What?"

"Why do you think the Amazons have endured for so many centuries? They need demigods, and I provide, from time to time."

"Does my mother know this?"

"Yes, unfortunately."

"And she agreed to trapping me here?"

"No. She was against it, but it doesn't matter. What's done is done."

"Of course, it matters," Deimos said. "It matters very much to know how much pain and suffering a parent is willing to inflict on a child."

"You're not a child, Deimos, so quit acting like one."

"Get me out of here. Set me free."

"I came to tell you that the rebels have taken your brothers and Psyche."

"Good."

"You think they're better off with Hades?"

"I do."

"Do you not care about the future of Mount Olympus?"

"I care more about my family."

"Mount Olympus *is* your family."

"Not anymore."

Ares balled his fists at his side. "If Mount Olympus falls, we all do. Think about that for the next two weeks."

Ares flew from the pit.

Deimos said nothing as the queen of the Amazons tugged on her rope to be lifted out.

Ellie clung to the side of Hades's chariot as Persephone drove, beneath the helm of invisibility, through the deep chasm of the Underworld toward the evening sky. Ellie and Phobos sat in the front with Persephone, while Cupid and Psyche rode in back. No one spoke a word as wisps of snow fell from the clouds and landed in their hair and on their clothes.

As they flew, Ellie wondered how Phobos really felt about the paternity of her twins. To Ellie, it was the best news she could have received, because it meant that neither god would be hurt—at least not completely. Phobos may wish to have her and the twins all to himself. She hoped, if that were the case, that she and Deimos could convince him to live together—all five of them—as a family.

According to Persephone, the perimeter of Demeter's winter cabin on Mount Kronos was heavily warded, but, nonetheless, she parked the chariot inside, to make it less conspicuous. Cupid unbridled Swift and Sure—the two black stallions—and put them in a room with hay that Hecate had already conjured.

"I'm so sorry," Ellie said to Hecate. "I'm the one who asked you to bring the helm to the ranch in the first place."

"I have a spell for those cuffs," Hecate said.

"Seriously?" Ellie beamed. "Oh, what fantastic news! I can't wait to be rid of them!"

"First, let's get everyone sorted and settled," Hecate said.

"It's good to see you up and about," Phobos said to Hecate.

"Thank you," she said. "It's good to *be* up and about."

"No one's more relieved than I," another goddess—*Demeter*, Ellie believed.

"Oh, Mother," Persephone teased. "Don't start."

A black Doberman lay curled before the fire beside what appeared to be a weasel. The dog lifted its head and said, "She can't help herself, and I know just how she feels."

"Let me show you to your rooms," Hecate said. "This way."

Ellie followed Hecate down a hall to a modest bedroom—much smaller than the suite in Cupid's castle but better than the west Texas shack. It was about the same size as Ariadne's room in the labyrinth, though the furnishings were rustic—as one would expect of a mountain cabin—and there was no natural basin.

"You and Phobos can stay here," Hecate said. "That is, I assume you want to be together?"

Ellie glanced at Phobos. "Of course, we do. Don't we?"

"Absolutely."

"Cupid and Psyche, you can take the one across the hall," Hecate said. "There's only one guest bathroom, I'm afraid, with a stand-up shower—no tub—but at least you can get cleaned up and get some rest, as I'm sure you're tired."

"Thank you," Psyche said. "I call dibs on the shower."

Hecate then followed Ellie and Phobos into their room and said, "Now for those cuffs. I've got everything we need over here, dear."

Ellie followed Hecate to a small wooden table, which had been laid out with four lit candles, a bowl filled with herbs, and a large glass jar. At the bottom of the jar was a single egg.

"Have a seat," Hecate said, pointing to one of the two chairs at the table. "You, too, Phobos."

Once they were seated, Hecate set fire to the bowl of herbs and washed the smoke over Ellie. Then she opened the glass jar, took out the egg, and poked a tiny hole on one end. To the egg, Hecate sprinkled the hot ash from the bowl and said, "I call the elements to my aid and offer up this simple egg. Banish the cuffs that hold my friend, so her imprisonment may end."

Ellie gasped when the cuffs cracked in half.

Hecate peeled them from Ellie's wrists and placed them inside the glass jar with the egg. Then she secured the lid and said, "I need to bury this in the earth, or the shackles will return. Get some rest."

Hecate blew out the candles and added, "It won't be long before the babies come. I can feel it."

Ellie hopped up and threw her arms around Hecate. "Thank you! Thank you, so much!"

"If I drop this jar and it breaks, the spell will reverse," Hecate warned.

Ellie stepped back. "I'm sorry. Of course."

The goddess of witchcraft left the room without another word.

Once they were alone, Phobos took her into his arms. "I'm glad to finally be alone with you."

She sighed and leaned against him. "Me, too."

He lifted her chin with his finger. "What did you mean when you said you'd never cut me out of the equation? Were you saying that you've made your choice? If so, listen to me. I knew you'd pick me. I had a feeling. Our chemistry is so incredible. But Deimos won't be able to handle this. This will crush him."

"It wouldn't crush *you*, if things went the other way?" Ellie asked.

"Of course, it would, but I'm stronger than my brother."

Ellie wasn't so sure about that, but Phobos's willingness to sacrifice his happiness for his brother made her love him all the more.

"Deimos thought of a solution," Ellie said with a grin. "I hope you'll consider it."

"What kind of solution?"

"What if I love you *both*? What if I don't choose? What if the three of us…"

Phobos cocked his head to the side. "What? How would *that* work?"

"Like that time in Circe's tree," she said, suddenly apprehensive. "That was nice, wasn't it? Couldn't the two of you *share* me?"

Phobos's mouth hung open as he stared at her, speechless.

"Give it some thought," she said. "We don't have to decide anything now."

Ellie wondered how long Phobos planned to sulk. He hadn't touched her in the entire week he'd been there with her, nor had he prayed or spoken about his feelings. He'd slept in the bed, and she'd lain beside him, stroking his back, but he kept his thoughts and his passions to himself.

He was asleep the day his powers came back. She lay in bed beside him, watching in awe as the luminosity returned to his skin, and his muscles and other features sharpened.

He opened his eyes, brighter in their godly form and as blue as a cloudless sky. "Now that my powers are back, I need to get my brother."

"Deimos?" she asked.

"Yes."

"How?"

He said, "I'm going to steal the helm."

Suddenly, Deimos appeared in the room with Artemis beside him, holding the helm.

"No need, brother. I'm back."

Deimos grinned when Ellie sprang from the bed and wrapped her arms around his neck.

"How did you get rid of your cuffs?" he asked.

"Hecate knows a spell. I'm sure she'll help you, too, but first tell me how you escaped."

"I'll let you tell her," Artemis said before she vanished beneath the helm.

"They let me go," Deimos said.

"Why?" Phobos asked.

Deimos told them about the queen of the Amazons, the breeder named Sonja, and the conditions of his release.

"They made you have sex with her?" Ellie stepped back.

"More than once, I think. I was drugged. It's all a blur."

"And you're having a daughter—a mortal daughter," Phobos said.

"It got me thinking," Deimos said to Ellie. "Maybe your father never knew you existed, or maybe he didn't have a choice about leaving you. Hecate could help us to find him—your sister's father, too."

"There's a lot going on," Phobos said. "Maybe later, after this conflict is over?"

"I guess I'd like to know the truth," Ellie said. "But there's no rush. I've waited this long. Maybe we should focus on the twins right now and what we're going to do, going forward, assuming we survive the reckoning."

"You're right," Deimos said. "Let's focus on that."

He didn't mention that he'd already asked Hecate to look into it for him.

Phobos got up from the bed. "There's something we need to tell you, bro'."

Deimos did not like the look on his brother's face or the vibe he was picking up from his brother's demeanor. "Uh-oh. Has something happened?"

"Maybe you should sit down," Phobos said, pointing to the table.

Deimos searched Ellie's face. *What the hell is going on?* He'd begun to fear that Ellie had chosen Phobos.

It's not bad, she replied telepathically. *Phobos has mixed feelings, but I think you'll be pleased.*

"Are you two talking behind my back?" Phobos asked.

"Spit it out," Deimos said to Phobos.

"You and I are *both* going to be fathers," Phobos said.

Deimos frowned and slumped over in his chair, resting his elbows on the table. If they were *both* going to be father's, then Ellie's twins must belong to Phobos.

He'd been so sure that he was the father. He could sense it. The disappointment was almost paralyzing.

"Congratulations," Deimos said. "I'm happy for you, brother."

"Wait," Ellie said. "I don't think you heard him right."

"Bro', I said we're *both* going to be fathers. I thought, after what Ellie said about a threesome, that you'd be happy for me."

"I am, Phobos," Deimos said. "Just disappointed for myself. I am allowed to be disappointed."

Deimos was fighting tears—not because he thought Ellie would reject him. He knew she loved him and, if they could get Phobos on board, would include him in her life; but, his confidence in sharing her came with the belief that *he* was the father of her twins. Now, he felt like an outsider. He supposed if the shoe were on the other foot, his brother would feel the same. He was stronger than Phobos and could handle it better. It was better this way.

But, gods, could the Fates be cruel.

"Deimos!" Ellie cried. "You don't get it."

"Her twins are fraternal," Phobos said. "Each with its own egg and sperm. One baby belongs to you and the other to me—though I don't know how we'll know which is which."

"Will it matter?" Ellie asked.

"No. It won't. I'll love them equally, I'm sure."

Deimos leapt to his feet. "Let me get this straight."

He ran their words through his mind again. He and his brother had fertilized a different egg. Ellie was carrying a child from each of them.

He wrapped his arms around Ellie. "What a relief. Oh, gods, what a relief!"

"Would it have made a difference?" she asked, pulling away to search his face.

"I don't know. Maybe. I suppose I would have felt a little like an outsider."

"And you no longer feel that way?" Phobos asked.

"Why? Should I?" he glanced at Ellie before returning his gaze to his brother.

Phobos began to pace the room. "No. Of course not. It's just that when I thought the babies were mine, and mine alone, I was willing to give Ellie up for you, because I felt like I'd still have a special connection to her as the father of her children. But now that our paternal connection is equal, well, it changes things."

Deimos crossed his arms at his chest, not sure he understood correctly. "You're saying you were going to bow out and let me have the love of your life?"

"It was easier than listening to you whine and complain for the rest of our lives—or so I thought," Phobos said.

"I can't believe you'd even consider such a thing," Deimos said.

"Neither can I," Ellie said.

"You mean to say you *didn't?*" Phobos asked Deimos. "You never thought about letting *me* have her?"

"I thought of a different solution," Deimos said, "based on the same reason as you."

"I heard."

"You don't approve?" Deimos asked.

"I don't know. What if, down the road, she ends up liking one of us better than the other? Won't that hurt?"

"Losing her *then* wouldn't hurt any more than losing her *now,*" Deimos reasoned.

"Are you sure about that?"

"No one's going to lose me," Ellie said.

"How can you know?" Phobos asked. "Don't you see what a tenuous position that would put us in—my brother and me? You'd have all the power, Ellie. We'd be at your mercy, afraid that if we put one toe out of line…"

"I'd marry you both," Ellie said. "I'd take an oath."

"Can three souls make such a vow?" Deimos asked.

"Yes," Ellie said. "More and more polygamous marriages are happening every day. I've read about this. It's a real thing. It's not recognized legally everywhere, but polyamorous people are making spiritual commitments to one another, just like couples do in monogamous marriages. Why can't we?"

"You'd really take an oath?" Phobos asked. "Not on the River Styx—I would never ask you to go that far—but an oath before the other gods? Because it's not the sharing that bothers me; it's the possibility of being pushed out."

"I wouldn't hesitate to take the oath," Ellie said. "I love you both with all my heart. And I want both of you involved in the daily lives of our babies. I want us to be a family together. And I would never push you out."

Deimos noticed his brother's eyes fill with tears.

"We can do this," Deimos told him. "I believe in us."

Phobos wiped his eyes. "Ellie stays in the middle at all times in the bed, bro'."

"I've already stipulated that," Deimos said with a grin.

"And we need to nail down more guidelines," Phobos said. "For example, will sex always involve all three of us, or can Deimos and I have one-on-one time with you?"

"As long as the one-on-one time is divided equally between us, I'd be okay with that," Deimos said.

"Ellie?" Phobos asked.

"I agree, though I must admit that I'm happiest when I'm with you both, like the time in Circe's hollowed-out tree."

"That was nice," Phobos said.

"When I was trapped in the Amazonian Pit," Deimos said, "that memory—and others, but mostly that one—got me through the long days and nights."

"When I'm with the two of you, the effects of fear and panic not only balance out but add to my feelings of contentment somehow. It's not as strong as it was when I was a mortal, but I can still feel it. It's an amazing feeling for me, still."

Deimos rarely felt flabbergasted, but that's what he felt in that moment. "It feels strangely as though this were meant to be."

"Should we give it another try?" Ellie suggested with a gleam in her eyes.

"Shouldn't I get these cuffs removed first?" Deimos asked.

"Do you really want to wait, bro'?"

"No. Not another second."

Ellie climbed into the bed, overjoyed to have her loves beside her. She peeled off her clothes, and Phobos and Deimos, being more experienced gods, made their clothes vanish.

"When will I remember to do things the easy way?" Ellie said with a laugh.

"It's fun watching you squirm out of them," Phobos said.

Deimos turned her to face him. "I prefer it that way, too."

"So far, so good, then" she said.

Deimos cupped her face and gave her his soft, slow, seductive kisses while Phobos cupped her breasts and pressed himself against her, arousing every inch of her. Then Phobos turned her to face him, and, as he ravished her mouth with his, Deimos grabbed her hip and entered her from behind.

She moved her hands down Phobos's chest until she found what she was looking for. She glided her hands up and down, and while Deimos brought her to the edge of climax, she brought Phobos there, too.

"I can't hold it any longer," she whispered.

Phobos pinched her nipple as he cried out, "Me, either."

Deimos gasped against her back. She could feel that it was the same for him.

Tears sprang to her eyes as her body exploded with pleasure.

"That was fast," she said between breaths. "Are you guys okay?"

"Amazing," Phobos said.

"Ditto," Deimos said. "We'll get better at making it last longer. Don't worry."

"I'm not worried. Let's just lie here together for as long as we can," Ellie said. "Hypnos helped me to sleep for three weeks straight, and yet I feel I could easily fall asleep again, because of how content I am."

"I have an idea," Phobos said.

"Now, that's something new," Deimos teased.

"Let's get married," Phobos said. "Before the babies are born. There's no way of knowing when they'll come."

"Seriously?" Just when Ellie didn't think she could be happier, she felt happier.

"The three of us?" Deimos asked, propping himself up on one elbow.

"No, Deimos," Phobos said sardonically. "I've decided to break your heart."

"No need to get sarcastic, brother. Just making sure we're on the same page."

"For someone who says he's so smart, you aren't so smart, bro'. Like I'd cut you out and propose with you right here. Come on, dude."

"Can't a god be *shocked?*" Deimos asked defensively. "I was *in shock*. You didn't seem keen on the idea not fifteen minutes ago."

"Boys, boys!" Ellie sat up in bed. "As much as I enjoy your banter, this isn't turning out to be the greatest marriage proposal."

"I'm sorry, Ellie," Phobos said.

"Sweet, Ellie," Deimos said. "Phobos, we need to do this properly."

Deimos snapped his fingers and suddenly he and Phobos were wearing tuxedos. Although they were super-hot without clothes, the tuxedos looked damn good on them.

"Nice touch, bro'," Phobos said.

Then Phobos snapped his fingers and a small black box appeared in his hand.

"I suppose she'll need two rings," Deimos said as a box appeared in his.

Ellie giggled while the two boys knelt on the floor at the foot of the bed.

"Ellie Beaufort," Phobos began.

"Will you do us the honor," Deimos said, then he looked over at his brother and cleared his throat.

"Of marrying us?" Phobos said.

"And making us the happiest gods alive?" Deimos added.

Ellie flew between them and wrapped an arm around each of them. "Yes! Yes, yes, yes!!"

CHAPTER TEN

Wedding Plans

I don't know about the rest of you," Demeter said, "but a wedding would certainly lift my spirits."

"But a wedding of *three*?" Artemis asked. "Is that allowed among the gods?"

Ellie sat on the sofa in Demeter's living room between Phobos and Deimos. Demeter and Hecate sat across from them in wingback chairs beside the hearth. Demeter wore her golden hair braided into the shape of a crown on her head. Hecate wore her black and white hair down across her back. The dog and weasel lay on a rug at Hecate's feet. Cupid and Psyche shared a loveseat, positioned at a right angle to both the couch and Hecate's chair and directly across the room from the dining table, where Artemis sat with a chair turned to face the others.

"There's no rule against it," Psyche said. "Not that I'm aware of. Cupid?"

"Hera would be the final authority on that question," he said, "but I've not heard of one either."

"We can't involve Hera," Artemis said, pointing out the obvious. "Unless you want to wait until this conflict is over, assuming the pantheon survives."

"We don't want to wait," Phobos said.

"And why should we?" Deimos asked. "We're just passing time out here, aren't we? Waiting for the twins to arrive, so we can keep them safe? We may as well make the best of it."

Ellie smiled first at Deimos and then at Phobos.

"What of your parents?" Hecate asked Phobos and Deimos. "Once this reckoning is concluded, assuming we survive, you may want to reconcile with them. Will you regret not having them present on your special day?"

"They can go to Tartarus," Phobos said. "Or, better yet, the Titan Pit."

Deimos shrugged. "That's a good point, Hecate. I do believe there's a chance for reconciliation."

"Come on, bro'. Seriously?"

"Let me finish," Deimos said. "But having them at the wedding isn't important to me."

"What about you?" Demeter asked Ellie. "Don't you want your mother here?"

Ellie took a deep breath as tears filled her eyes. "Yes, to be honest. It would mean a lot to me to have my mother and sister here. But is that even possible?"

"It is," Hecate said. "It's also possible to have your father here, if you'd like to meet him."

Ellie turned to Deimos with wide eyes.

"That was quick," Deimos said to Hecate.

"I used one of Ellie's boots," Hecate said. "I'll need something of Dominique's to find *her* father."

"I'd asked her to look before checking with you," Deimos explained to Ellie. "Sorry."

"No, it's okay," she said. "I think I would like to meet him. I just don't know yet if I want him at my wedding."

"That's easily solved," Demeter pointed out. "Hecate can take the helm and bring him here, if you'd like. She can take him home, if you don't want him to stay for the ceremony."

"Really?" Ellie asked, suddenly nervous, but also excited, about the idea.

Hecate nodded. "I'll have to wipe his memory, as I will your mother's and sister's, so they don't accidentally give away our location to a loyalist in a prayer."

"Oh," Ellie said. "I guess that's fine."

"I can restore their memories after the conflict is over," Hecate said. "Assuming I'm not thrown into the Titan Pit, or worse. Okay, dear?"

Ellie nodded her thanks.

Artemis turned the helm over to Hecate. "Sounds like we have a plan."

"Great," Demeter said. "Now, let's discuss flower arrangements. Oh, but my dear Persephone will want to help with that. Hecate, can you bring her back with you, when you deliver Ellie's father?"

"I certainly can," Hecate said before she put on the helm and disappeared.

Cupid stood from the loveseat. "She left before I could ask to tag along."

Phobos cocked his head to the side. "Why would you want to do that?"

"I feel like a caged animal," Cupid replied.

Deimos shook his head. "No, no, no, no, brother. Spend a month in the Amazonian Pit, and *then* you can complain."

"Sounds like it wasn't *all* bad," Psyche said as she twirled a strand of her dark hair around a finger.

Ellie's face grew hot.

"Let's go for a walk, Cupid," Deimos said. "We need to talk."

Glad to be rid of his adamantine cuffs, which Hecate had removed with a spell earlier that day, Deimos led Cupid through the backdoor of Demeter's cabin, to walk the perimeter. He glanced at the surrounding trees for the wards and made sure to remain within the circle of protection.

"What's up?" Cupid asked.

"You need to talk to Psyche. What she said back there wasn't cool."

"I know. She's still sore about being stripped of her powers."

"Ellie was trying to help. Things could have been worse."

"Psyche doesn't think so."

"She got to be with you, didn't she?" Deimos pointed out.

"She thinks she would have, anyway, beneath the helm."

"You know that's impossible, right? The rebels have needed that helm nearly every day that you've been gone."

"I suppose you're right."

"Talk to her," Deimos said. "Will you? Get her to see the light? I can tell it's been hard on Ellie."

"I'll try, but I can't promise anything."

"That's all I'm asking."

They continued to circle the perimeter for a few minutes in silence.

Then Cupid asked, "How do you feel about becoming a father?"

Deimos grinned. "Excited. If you'd asked me before all of this, I would have said that fatherhood was the very last thing I wanted, but I would have been wrong. I'm looking forward to it." Then he added, "I'm having two girls, you know? One mortal. I want to be a part of her life, too."

"I hope it works out, brother. I really do."

Phobos squeezed Ellie's hand. "You okay?"

She took a deep breath. "I think so."

"You seem nervous."

"I am."

"You want to be alone for this, when your father gets here?" he asked.

Ellie smiled up at him. "I guess so."

Hecate appeared with the helm, Persephone, and a mortal man—a white man.

Ellie climbed to her feet. "Who's this?"

"Ellie Beaufort, this is James Lorenzo. James, this is your daughter, Ellie, born to Alice Beaufort."

"Where am I?" James asked.

"There must be some mistake," Ellie said to Hecate. "My father is black."

"There's no mistake," Hecate said. "This man is your father. He was one of your mother's customers when she worked the streets of New Orleans. Isn't that right, James?"

"Who the hell are you?" he asked Hecate.

"I'm one of the goddesses of the Underworld," Hecate said. "You've been given a chance, before your death, to make amends with your daughter, Ellie."

James blinked and raked his fingers though his dark hair. It was gray at the temples.

"Let's give them the room," Demeter said to the other gods. "Persephone, dear, let's discuss the flower arrangements in my sitting room."

Phobos gave Ellie a pat on the shoulder. "Just call if you need me."

Ellie was still trying to process Hecate's words, trying to absorb the fact that this white man was her father. Her mother had told her that he was black.

"Thanks," she said to Phobos.

Once the others had left the room, James asked, "What the hell is going on?"

"Let's sit down," Ellie said, trying to hide her trembling hands.

She led him to the dining table, so they could sit across from one another. Still in shock, she studied his features. He had wavy dark hair and dark eyes, and, although he was white, his skin wasn't pale. He was handsome and, like her mother, appeared to be in his late forties.

"Is this a dream?" he asked.

"In a way, it is," she said. "Do you remember Alice Beaufort?"

"That was a long time ago."

"Twenty-one years ago," Ellie said.

"Look, if you're really my daughter, don't take this personally, but she was a whore—a prostitute—you hear? She wasn't in love with me any more than I was in love with her. And I was a married man, you get it? I had a family already. You would think a woman in her profession would learn to use birth control."

"It's not a hundred-percent foolproof," Ellie said. "And you would think a man like you, who cheated on his wife, would learn to use it, too. Did you?"

"That was years ago. You expect me to remember?"

"You remember. Be honest with me. I deserve that much."

"I was young. I was stupid."

"But Alice was the one who had to pay. You did nothing to support her."

"I offered to pay for an abortion."

"And when she told you she was having the baby, what did you do?" Ellie asked.

"I told her I didn't want to have any part of it," he said.

"Why do men think they can do that?" Ellie was shaking. "That mistake belonged to *both* of you, and so did the consequences. It's easy for a man to say to get an abortion, but it's not easy for the woman. You should have helped her."

"What's the difference? You're all grown up now."

"I hope the Furies torture you in Tartarus."

"Whoa. Torture? What are you talking about? You said I could go home. Am I dead?"

"Not yet, unfortunately." Then Ellie said, "Tell me about your family."

"There's not much to tell."

"Then it shouldn't take long," Ellie pointed out.

"My wife and I divorced years ago. We had a son, but we haven't kept in touch."

"What do you do for a living?" she asked.

"I own several apartment complexes and small single-family units in some areas of New Orleans," he said. "Not in the wealthiest areas, but I do okay."

"You're a slum lord?" she asked.

"I prefer the term landlord."

Tears filled her eyes. She couldn't be more disappointed in the man sitting before her.

"Can I go home now?" he asked. "Or do I just need to wake up?" He laughed. "How does this work?"

Then she had an idea.

Hecate, she prayed. *Can we make James stay for the wedding? I'd like my mother to have a chance to give him a piece of her mind. That would be oh, so satisfying to watch.*

Hecate appeared. "Come with me, James. I'll show you to your room."

"What?" he asked. "I thought I could go home."

"First you need to go back to sleep," Hecate said. To Ellie, she prayed, *I'll have Hip put this man into the deep boon of sleep until tomorrow— after the ceremony, if you'd like. Your mother can have it out with him then.*

Perfect, Ellie said. *Thank you.*

Back in Demeter's guest room, Deimos sat at the wooden table across from the bed, while Phobos stared at himself in a mirror that hung over a dresser.

"What are you doing?" Deimos asked.

"I've just written a song for the wedding about tortillas—actually, it's more of a rap."

"Seriously."

"I got used to the beard on the ranch, dude. I can't decide if I want to keep it for the ceremony."

"Have you asked Ellie?"

"She says she likes me either way."

"Then keep it," Deimos said.

"Why? *You* don't wear one."

"It'll make it that much easier for people who are on the fence about which of us is better looking. Keep the beard, and I'll shine in comparison."

Phobos laughed. "You suck, bro'. I might just keep it anyway." Then he added, "Don't you hate it when someone answers their own question? I do."

"You're hilarious, Phobos."

"Don't state the obvious, Professor Deimos."

"Listen," Deimos said. "What do you think about asking Cupid to be our best man?"

"I was thinking the same thing. It would prove to him that we've forgiven him. I'm so sick of his whiny prayers."

"Exactly," Deimos said.

"Besides, who else would we ask?"

The brothers laughed.

After Ellie had returned to the guest room in Demeter's cabin to tell the boys what had happened with her biological father, they brightened her spirits by telling her that they'd asked Cupid to be their best man and that Cupid had agreed.

"I'm glad the three of you are okay again," she said. "I know it wasn't my fault, but I felt like it was—the rift between you."

"You brought us closer together," Deimos said.

"I wouldn't go that far," Phobos said with a laugh. "But, yeah, it's all good."

"Who will stand with *you*?" Deimos asked Ellie.

She hadn't even thought about it. She sat on the edge of the bed. "I don't know."

"No worries. The wedding isn't for another five or six hours," Phobos said, laughing again.

"Guys, what am I going to do? My sister and I aren't close. I love her and miss her, but I never felt like she cared much about me. She was always doing her own thing. And Shaylynn, well, I don't think I want to ask her *here*."

"What about Psyche?" Deimos said. "She was the one who saved your life."

"She's the reason we're together," Phobos added. "That, and my good looks."

Ellie laughed.

"See?" Phobos said to Deimos. "She agrees. It's the beard, bro'."

Deimos shook his head. "Only *you* would mistake laughter for agreement."

"I'm so happy to see you two back to your usual selves," Ellie said. "But here's the thing: As much as I love and admire her, as grateful as I feel to her, Psyche hates me."

"She did have a few choice words for you that time she slipped into a pile of horse shit," Phobos said.

"You're not helping, Phobos," Deimos said.

"Laughter is the best medicine, dude. Ellie likes it when I make her laugh."

Deimos took Ellie's hands. "Talk to her. You can't avoid her forever."

"Okay," she said. "Here goes nothing."

"Why do people say that?" Phobos said. "It's not nothing. It's something. You should say: Here goes something."

Ellie laughed. "Fine! Here goes *something!*"

She left the room and went across the hall, where she knocked on Psyche and Cupid's bedroom door.

Psyche answered. "I may have been eavesdropping."

"Oh. Can we talk?" Ellie asked.

Psyche took Ellie by the hand and led her down the hall, through the main room, and out the front door.

"Is it safe out here?" Ellie asked.

"As long as we stay in the circle of protection. See that tree?"

Ellie followed Psyche's finger. "Yeah?"

"There's a sigil on the trunk. See it? That symbol that's like a half-moon?"

"Oh, yeah. I see it."

"All the trees around the cabin are marked, but we should stay vigilant, just in case."

"Okay." Ellie kept her eyes on the trees in the distance.

"I want to apologize," Psyche said.

"You don't need to apologize! I'm the one who's sorry."

"Ellie, none of this has been your fault. You're the innocent in all of this. And what you did on Mount Olympus may have saved me from a worse fate."

"You really think so?"

"I didn't at first," Psyche admitted. "But now that I've heard all the stories…"

"What stories?"

"The Underworld was attacked. Meg—one of the Furies—was captured."

"What?"

"Zeus nearly swallowed her, but Hermes intervened and saved her."

"Hermes?"

"Yes. He returned her to the Underworld. If he hadn't been there…"

"Oh, my gods."

"I know."

They continued walking around the cabin for a few minutes while Ellie processed what she'd just been told.

When they reached the point where they'd begun, in front of the cabin, Ellie asked, "So, I know things have been tense between us lately.

I hope you know how grateful I am to you for saving my life when Aphrodite wanted to kill me."

"She wanted to kill me once, too," Psyche said.

"You've always been on my side. You were my first immortal friend. It would mean the world to me if you'd be my matron of honor. Will you, Psyche?"

"I'd be happy to," she said.

Ellie gave the goddess a hug as tears pricked her eyes. "I will always be grateful to you."

Psyche hugged her back. "We girls have to watch out for one another."

CHAPTER ELEVEN

Marriage on the Mountain

Ellie paced in Demeter's living room as she waited for the arrival of her mother and sister. She hoped they'd be happy for her and not disappointed. She hoped they wouldn't oppose her marriage to two people, since it was far from traditional.

What was traditional, anyway? Her mother and sister had families *without* partners. And other people had multiple partners, just not *simultaneously*. Was it necessarily better to marry two or three people consecutively?

She hoped that one day, after the conflict with the gods, if she wasn't imprisoned somewhere, that her family could know the truth about her life as a goddess and share in the benefits of it. Ellie wanted to give her family a big house and nice cars and all the money they could ever want so they could be happy and not have to struggle every day of their lives. She hoped with all her heart that she could do that for them.

She also hoped that her mother would give her away at the ceremony, since there was no way Ellie would ever consider asking James Lorenzo.

The more she thought about James, the more upset she became—especially when she considered his lack of regret. He never once said he was sorry or that he'd wondered about her or that he'd hoped the best for her. He'd put her and her mother out of his mind and had forgotten all about them.

Her stomach dropped when Hecate appeared with her mother and sister. Her mother was wearing her new, short wig, with the ends curled up, and Dominique's long hair was French braided in a single braid down her back.

"What on earth?" her mother cried, looking around. Then she spotted Ellie. "Ellie? Is that really you?"

"It's really me, Mama."

"How did we get here? What's happening?" Dominique asked.

"I'll explain everything," Ellie said. "Please have a seat."

Hecate vanished, causing Ellie's mother to scream.

"Sit down, Mama," Ellie said.

"You're pregnant!" Dominique said as she sat beside their mother on Demeter's couch. "When did that happen? It looks like you're ready to pop! Is this why you haven't come home? I bet you didn't know that I'm expecting, too."

"Congratulations, Dominique." Ellie sat on the loveseat. "This is going to be hard for you to believe, but please listen. Have you ever heard of Zeus and Poseidon and those gods from ancient Greece?"

"Like Aphrodite?" Dominique asked.

"Yes," Ellie said. "Well, they're real. They exist. The goddess who brought you here is one of them. Her name is Hecate."

Dominique looked at their mama, and their mama looked at Dominique. Then the two of them busted out laughing.

After a moment, her mother said, "Tell us what's really going on."

"I'm getting married," Ellie said.

"Seriously?" Dominique asked. "Who is this guy, and why haven't we ever met him?"

"It's not *a guy*, actually."

"Oh," Dominique said. "I always thought you might be a lesbian."

Ellie shook her head. "It's not a woman, either. It's *two* guys. Two *gods*."

"Can you quit with all the god talk?" her mother said. "You don't have to make up stories to defend your polygamous lifestyle. You were never one to lie, so why start now?"

Frustrated, Ellie pointed her finger at the hearth and made the fire die. Then she brought the fire back to life.

"What on earth?" her mother said.

Then Ellie flew around the room. Her mother fainted. Dominique started crying.

"Tell me I'm dreaming," Dominique said through trembling lips. "This can't really be happening." She patted their mother's cheeks. "Mama, wake up! Mama!"

Ellie's mother came to and stared at Ellie, who hovered above them in the air.

"Listen to me," Ellie said. "I'm a goddess. My future husbands are gods. I'm having twin daughters who will also be gods. I'm getting married today, and I want you to be at the ceremony."

Her mother, who looked as though she'd seen a ghost, muttered, "Whatever you say."

Ellie prayed to Phobos and Deimos to join her. They walked in and stood beside Ellie in front of the couch, where Ellie said, "Mama and Dominique, this is Deimos, the god of panic, and Phobos, the god of fear. Guys, this is Alice and Dominique Beaufort."

"It's a pleasure to meet you," Deimos said, extending a hand.

The two women looked at him with wide eyes. Her mother became as still as a statue and appeared to be holding her breath. Dominique ran toward the door, but Phobos caught her.

"We have that effect on people," Phobos said. Then he turned to El-lie. "We'll leave you to it."

The two gods disappeared, and Ellie's mother screamed again.

"Maybe this was a mistake," Ellie muttered.

Her mother stood from the couch and touched Ellie's cheek. "Is it really you, baby girl?"

"Yes, Mama. I've missed you."

Her mother put her arms around Ellie's waist. "I've been so worried about you."

"I'm okay."

Her mother stepped back and looked at her belly. "When are you due?"

"I'm not sure. It could be any day now."

"And one of those men—er, gods—is the father?"

"They're both the father. I'm having two girls—one by each of them."

"Hmm." Her mother seemed to be soaking it all in.

Dominique sat, crying, on the couch, also trying to process it all.

"Mama?" Ellie asked.

"Yes?"

"Would you give me away at the wedding, since I don't have a father to do it?"

"You don't need a father, or anyone, to give you away. I never understood that tradition, to tell you the truth. Why someone got to give you away? You don't belong to anyone but yourself. You can give yourself away."

Ellie had never thought of it like that before. She smiled. "You're right, Mama. I can give myself away. But you'll stay for the ceremony?"

"Of course, I will. Just give me a beat to get used to it all."

"There's not much time," Ellie said. "Will you come and help me with my wedding dress?"

Dominique climbed to her feet. "I'm sorry I'm freaking out. It's just so…freaky."

Ellie hugged her sister. "I know it is. Come on."

Ellie led her mother and sister down the hall to the guest room. When she opened the door, Demeter and Persephone were waiting with a lovely gown in their arms.

Ellie introduced them, and then the gown appeared on her body. Her mother and sister jumped.

"What on earth?" her mother exclaimed.

"That's how gods get dressed, Mama," Ellie said. "Try to relax and calm down."

Persephone snapped her fingers to make the dress on Ellie transform with a different skirt, and then other, changing the length, width, and colors—ranging from stark white to creamy ivory. They also changed the bodice and neckline and sleeves. Ellie felt like a video game character.

Her mother and sister seemed to adjust, because, at one point, her mother said, "Go back to the last one," of the bodice.

Persephone snapped her fingers. "This one?"

"That's the one," Ellie's mother said.

It had a v-neckline with no sleeves and pearl beading.

"And how about that puffy skirt," her mother said.

"I liked the fitted one," Dominique said. "The puffy one makes her look fat."

Ellie frowned.

"Only because you're pregnant, Ellie. I'm looking out for you, sis."

"This one?" Persephone asked Dominique.

"Yes," Ellie's sister said.

"That does look nice," Ellie's mother said. "I think that's the one."

"Me, too," Demeter said. "It's beautiful."

"*You're* beautiful, Ellie," Dominique said. "I'm really happy for you."

Ellie smiled, holding back tears. "Thank you." Then covered her mouth and asked, "What am I going to do for wedding rings?"

Persephone held out her palms, where a small box appeared in each. "Gifts from Hades and me. Rings of the finest gold."

The tears she was holding back ran down her cheeks. "I can't thank you enough."

Deimos, Phobos, and Cupid stood in their tuxedos before a stone altar, where Hecate, the presider of the ceremony, faced the wedding guests with her palms in the air. Nearby, Hermes played a wedding tune with his pipe while Psyche, dressed in a silky lavender gown and carrying a single white rose, made her way down a center aisle, lined with a red carpet and baskets of lovely white camelias, tied with ivory ribbon.

In white folding chairs in rows on each side of the aisle sat the gods and goddesses of the rebel alliance, save Hades and one of the Furies, who stayed behind to guard the Underworld. Ellie's mother and sister, dressed in fine clothes, courtesy of Persephone, sat together among the gods, looking as though they believed it was all a dream.

Once Psyche joined Deimos and his brothers near the altar, Ellie emerged from the back door of the cabin looking lovely in her ivory gown, its pearls and beads sparkling in the evening sunlight. She carried a bouquet of white roses as she stepped forward. Hermes changed his tune to the wedding march. The guests rose from their seats to turn and watch the lovely bride as she glided down the red carpet toward the altar.

Deimos's heart was beating fast, not because he was nervous, but because he had never been more excited in his life. The grin on his twin brother's face told him that Phobos was feeling the same.

Ellie blew kisses to her mother and sister as she passed them. While Deimos found it adorable, it made him wish his mother could be there, too. As hurt and upset as he was for all she had done to him, he still loved her.

And, if he was being honest with himself, he would have liked for his father to be there, too. Everything his parents were doing, they were doing because they believed it was for the good of the Olympians, and that included Deimos and his brothers. How could he fault his parents for wanting the same things as he but believing in a different approach to obtaining them?

When Ellie took her place between Deimos and Phobos, she smiled up at them. Her beautiful dark eyes were moist with tears ready to slip down her cheeks. Deimos's own eyes pooled with tears as he realized that, even in the midst of this horrific conflict, he could find such profound joy.

Hermes finished his song and took a seat in the first row as Hecate said, "We are gathered here today…"

Hecate was interrupted by gasps from wedding guests. Deimos turned to see Circe, the witch, walking toward them down the aisle on the red carpet.

"Why have you come?" Hecate asked from the altar.

"To claim what was promised to me," Circe shrieked.

The rasp in her witchy voice was always a surprise, because it came from such a beautiful face with bright glowing eyes surrounded by braids of bright yellow hair. One would think her voice would be as melodious as her appearance was bright, but she spoke as though her throat were full of gravel.

"And what was that?" Demeter asked as she joined Hecate near the altar.

"Ask Cupid," the witch said, pointing a finger at him.

Cupid's face paled. "I promised her a match. That horrible day on Mount Olympus, when I shot the arrows of hate at my brothers, I promised Circe a match in exchange for her cooperation."

"And you promised to deliver him when your sentence was over," Circe said. "It's been over six months, and I have no match."

Circe raised her arms in the air, causing the trees to sway around the perimeter. "If I don't get what I was promised, you will be sorry. I will tell Zeus where you are. I will rip these warded trees by their roots and expose you to your enemies, I will…"

"Please, Circe," Cupid cried. "This is between you and me. Let's not involve the others. Don't ruin my brothers' wedding day."

"What about *my* wedding day?"

One of the evergreens along the perimeter lifted into the sky, its roots spewing dirt at the crowd before the tree crashed on the mountainside.

"Wait!" Hecate said. "Cupid kept his promise. Your match is here, asleep, waiting for you."

Deimos wondered what Hecate was talking about. Then he remembered Ellie's biological father.

He prayed to Ellie, *Does Hecate mean your father?*

Ellie turned to him. *I hope so. That would be so awesome if he was stuck with Circe for the rest of his life.*

The witch will probably use dark magic to keep him alive.

Even better, Ellie prayed.

Cupid left and returned with James Lorenzo, who was still groggy from his long nap.

Circe looked pleased.

But, suddenly, Alice Beaufort was on her feet and stomping toward Circe's match.

"Is that James? James Lorenzo?" Alice asked. "What on earth are you doing here?"

"I don't really know," James replied.

"If I had a dime for every time I wished I could run into you like this and tell you what a dirt bag I think you are, I'd be as rich as you," Alice said.

Deimos noticed the wide grin that crossed Ellie's face as she watched her mother have her say.

"Watch your tone!" Circe shouted at Alice. "That's *my man* you're talking to!"

Ellie flew to her mother's side and escorted her back to her seat. "Don't worry, Mama. He's getting what he deserves."

As James gave Circe a bewildered look, Cupid shot him in the heart with an arrow of love before doing the same to Circe.

James sauntered over to Circe, took her in his arms, and said, "I've never seen anyone as beautiful as you."

For once, Circe's laughter sounded less like a cackle and more like a girlish giggle.

"Join us, Circe and James," Hecate said. "Join us at this wedding altar. I'll marry you, as well."

Never in a hundred centuries would Deimos have guessed that he'd one day share his wedding with Circe the witch, especially after that day in her window when she'd given him his scar; but he didn't care. He was elated once the vows were exchanged in front of the other gods and he could officially call Ellie his wife—and he was equally happy that his brother, whom he loved as much as Ellie, could do the same.

Ellie felt as if the universe were finally on her side as she danced with her husbands at the beautiful reception in Demeter's cabin, where food and wine and music and smiling guests were plentiful. Her mother and sister left early, because they needed to get Jonivan from his sitter, so Hecate gave Ellie one last moment to say goodbye before wiping their memories and returning them home.

The merriment continued after Circe and her new husband had left and after the Underworld gods, save Hecate, had returned to Hades. Hecate and Artemis, who had refrained from drinking, and Demeter, who was as drunk as a skunk, stayed, along with Cupid and Psyche, to guard the newlyweds. Ellie had limited herself to one glass of wine, because of the babies, but she'd told her husbands to drink as much as they wished, and they did.

Just now, dancing with her near Demeter's hearth with a goblet of wine, Phobos was saying, "One of my favorite mortals is a dentist who just died today. He's filling his last cavity! Bwhahaha!"

"That's actually funny, brother!" Deimos slapped Phobos on the back.

"Wait, here's another," Phobos said. "I overheard a mortal say that he dropped his phone in the street, but the phone wasn't damaged. You know why?"

"Why?" Ellie asked.

"It was on airplane mode!"

Deimos frowned. "What's airplane mode?"

"And you're supposed to be the professor? I thought your brain was full of useless information."

"Don't be so disappointed, brother," Deimos said, laughing. "You know what the dyslexics say: When life gives you melons…"

"Bwhahahaha!" Phobos cried.

Cupid and Psyche came up to them to say goodnight.

"It was a lovely ceremony, even with Circe's surprise appearance," Psyche said.

"Cupid saved the day," Phobos said.

Cupid shook his head. "That was Hecate's doing."

Ellie glanced across the room at Hecate, who was helping the drunken Demeter to walk from the room. "We're lucky to have her on our side."

"Congratulations again," Cupid said. "I can't tell you how relieved I am that it turned out well for you, brothers. I would have never forgiven myself, otherwise."

Deimos shook his brother's hand. "And now you have our gratitude."

"So, stop with the whiny prayers," Phobos teased.

After Cupid and Psyche headed for their room, Ellie said, "Should we turn in as well?"

Four blue eyes and two smiles sparkled back at her.

"I'll take that as a yes. Come on."

The boys were in a silly mood. They kissed and pinched and made her laugh, but she soon learned it wouldn't be a night of consummation—not that they needed it. Before long, the two of them were snoring loudly beside her with their mouths hanging open. She giggled and closed her eyes, thanking Hecate and the other gods who had contributed to her special day before allowing herself to drift to sleep.

"Oh, no." Phobos sat up.

"What's wrong?" Ellie blinked and stretched, wondering how long they'd been sleeping.

"Phobos?" Deimos asked.

"I just heard a prayer from Christina Garcia," he said. "Rose and Violet are missing."

CHAPTER TWELVE

Birth and Delivery

Ellie, Phobos, and Deimos flew out of bed and dressed themselves before they raced to Demeter's living room, in search of the other gods.

"Cupid?" Phobos called.

He appeared in an instant, with Psyche at his side.

"What's the matter?" Demeter asked from where she sat in a wingback chair near the hearth, apparently nursing a hangover.

Hecate sat in the other wingback across from her, with the dog and weasel curled on the rug at her feet. "Has something happened?"

Suddenly, Artemis appeared with the helm and two stuffed animals. "The Garcia children are missing. Danny prayed to me early this morning. They were taken during the night."

"By loyalists?" Ellie asked.

Phobos groaned. "They're retaliating."

Cupid raked his fingers through his golden curls. "When they found us missing, they must have taken the girls as leverage."

"My stomach feels sick." Ellie rubbed her belly, which was nearly the size of a volleyball.

"Can you do a location spell, Hecate?" Artemis asked.

Hecate crossed the room to Artemis. "I assume those toys belonged to the girls?"

Artemis nodded.

"Then yes. I need a map of the world, four blue candles, a silver bowl, water, and incense made of jasmine, lotus, thyme, or mesquite, and clippings from those toys."

Ellie watched in awe as the gods collected the things and laid them out on Demeter's dining table.

It wasn't long before smoke from the incense filled the room. Hecate poured water into the silver bowl. Next, she lit parts of the stuffed animals on fire before adding them to the bowl. Then she put a flame to the world map and, as she dropped it into the bowl with the rest, she said, "Show me the location of Rose and Violet Garcia."

The gods looked on as the flames in the bowl turned to smoke. Then Hecate reached into the water and pulled out what remained of the burned map. It was a small piece of paper, the size of a Post-It Note.

"Thessaly," Hecate said. "The loyalists have taken the girls to Mount Olympus."

"It's a trap," Artemis said. "They know how much the Garcia family means to me."

"What should we do?" Ellie asked.

Cupid crossed his arms over his chest. "Danny and Christina must be worried sick."

"Those poor little girls," Phobos said.

"I can't believe Zeus and the others would subject those innocents to this," Deimos said.

"I can," Psyche said.

"The gods wouldn't kill Rose and Violet, would they?" Ellie asked.

"I wouldn't put it past them," Cupid said. "They were going to kill you, remember?"

Ellie suddenly recalled that Cupid had considered killing her, too. "Oh, no."

Hecate waved her hand to clear off the table. "We need a plan."

Ellie slumped onto the couch and clutched her abdomen.

Phobos flew to her side. "Are you okay?"

"I don't feel well," Ellie said just as water poured down her legs. "Oh, my gods! My water broke!"

"What?" Deimos looked at her from across the room. "It's time? *Now?*"

"Help her to lie down," Hecate said as she flew across the room.

Ellie was scared. She could feel the twins pressing against her innards, as if they didn't know which way was out.

"Is everything okay?" Psyche asked Hecate.

"I believe so," Hecate said.

Ellie broke out in a sweat and felt woozy.

The weasel appeared at Hecate's side with fresh towels. One of them was damp.

"Put this on her forehead, to keep her cool," the weasel said to Deimos.

"Thanks, Galin," Deimos said.

"Galin used to be a midwife," Hecate said of the weasel. "She helped to deliver Hercules."

"Oh." Ellie braced herself for the pain. It was like a vice squeezing her entire trunk.

Artemis comforted her with a blanket. "You'll want to remove your clothes."

Ellie closed her eyes and focused on removing them. Then, she held the blanket over her, trying to have faith and hope that all would turn out well.

"Can I get you something?" Phobos asked. "Some cold water?"

Ellie nodded.

Deimos smoothed her hair from her face. "Everything's going to be okay, Ellie. We're all here to help."

When Phobos returned with the water, he held it to her lips for her to drink.

"You know," he began, "most women say that childbirth is the most painful time of their lives until about three years later, when they walk on Legos."

Ellie smiled. "Good one, Phobos, but if you say one more joke before the girls are born, I'll eat you alive."

Phobos grinned. "Promise?"

Ellie closed her eyes as the pain around her belly became sharp and intense. She felt beads of sweat dripping down her forehead.

Hecate lifted the blanket from Ellie's feet and folded it over her knees. "I see one of the babies crowning. Can you push, Ellie?"

Ellie bore down, grunting with the pain. It felt as if a donkey were kicking against her back, again and again.

"I thought this would be less painful as a goddess," Ellie cried when the pain let up. "Why does it hurt so damn much?"

"Your babies are larger than mortal infants," Artemis explained.

"The head is almost through," Hecate assured her.

"Oh, my gods," Phobos said from Ellie's feet. "I think I'm going to faint."

Ellie turned to Deimos. "Please make him shut up."

Deimos laughed, which only angered her.

"Push with the contraction, Ellie," the weasel named Galin said.

The pain built up. More donkeys kicked against her back. She thought she would break in two as she pushed with all her might.

"She's here!" Hecate said.

"She's beautiful!" Phobos said.

"Look at those golden wings!" Deimos cried.

With the lull in pain, Ellie said, "Can I see her?"

Artemis cleaned the baby with a towel and showed her to Ellie. The baby's skin was bronze and shiny. Her golden wings were tucked at her side. She had small black curls all over her head. Her eyes were closed but her mouth was open.

"Cupid, this is what the mortals think you look like," Ellie said, smiling. "A little cherub!"

Before Ellie could take her newborn in her arms, the donkey kicked against her back and the vice squeezed her abdomen again.

"Push!" Galin cried.

Ellie bore down and grunted.

"That was the first placenta," Hecate said. "With the next contraction. Push again."

It wasn't long before the vice squeezed, and the donkeys kicked. Ellie pushed and wailed with pain.

"That's it," Hecate said. "She's coming."

Deimos kissed Ellie's forehead and held her hand as she pushed again.

Phobos said, "Oh, my gods. She's beautiful!"

"She's out!" Hecate said. "You did it! Now push again to clear the other placenta."

"I want to see her!" Ellie cried as she pushed.

Psyche cleaned the second baby with a towel and showed her to Ellie.

"Golden wings, like her sister's," Deimos said.

"And bronze skin," Ellie said. "She's gorgeous."

"Look at her curly red hair," Phobos said. "I wonder who she got that from."

The baby blinked, revealing dark eyes.

Phobos and Deimos helped Ellie to sit up on the couch while Psyche and Artemis put each of the babies to Ellie's breasts. The babies were bigger than footballs but smaller than beachballs, and Ellie was able to hold them comfortably. Her husbands sat on either side of her, doting.

The dark-haired baby opened her eyes to reveal crystal blue eyes. Ellie smiled. One baby had her daddy's red hair and the other had her daddy's blue eyes—she just didn't know which came from which father. She hoped that wouldn't matter to them.

As for Ellie, she couldn't imagine being more fulfilled than she was in that moment.

Deimos couldn't stop staring at the two little bundles curled in Ellie's arms, nursing at her breasts.

Hecate came up from behind the couch and looked down at the babes. "This is probably the only time they'll drink from you, Ellie. Many immortal infants don't nurse at all."

"They seem to be growing by the second," Ellie said.

"They are," Phobos said.

"What should we name them?" Deimos asked.

They hadn't had a chance to discuss baby names.

"Faith and Hope," Ellie said. "Because that's what I need in my life to get through this reckoning."

The redhead wriggled from Ellie's arm and shook out her golden wings.

"Hope," Ellie said. "My sweet, darling girl. Your name is Hope."

Hope stretched out her wings and flew about the room until she plopped onto Deimos's lap. Before she could get away again, he held her firmly and kissed her cheek.

"You've been through a lot, little one," he said. "Just let me hold you for a bit."

The black-haired baby shook out her wings, too, and wiped her mouth with her tiny fist.

"Such a sweet, adorable girl," Ellie said. "Your name is Faith."

Like her sister, she was determined to test out her wings. She flew around the room and then gently landed in Phobos's arms.

Although the little cherubs were born in their birthday suits, Deimos gave them pretty dresses to wear.

"Don't make our girls look like Victorian baby dolls," Phobos complained, changing the lacey, frilly dresses into simpler ones, with a sailor's collar and blue ties.

"Adorable," Psyche said.

"Let's dress them in matching jumpsuits," Ellie said, switching them out. "Oh, they're so cute!"

"I think we've taken *playing dress up* to the next level," Phobos said with a laugh.

"It is kind of fun." Deimos held baby Hope on his lap and gazed into her dark eyes. "A different kind of fun than we're used to—wouldn't you agree, brother?"

"I can't believe this is happening," Phobos said. "I never thought I'd get to have this kind of life."

"Well, enjoy it while you can," Demeter said from across the room. "Because none of us knows what the future holds."

"How uplifting," Phobos said sardonically.

"I hate to break up this family moment," Artemis said, "But we have to come up with a plan to save the Garcia girls."

"I just had a terrible thought," Deimos said. "What if Zeus wants to make a trade for our twins?"

Ellie turned to him with a look of terror. "Oh, my gods. That's it, isn't it?"

Suddenly, Hermes appeared. "Deimos is right. Zeus is threatening to kill the little girls from west Texas, unless Ellie brings her babes to Mount Olympus."

In the next moment, with no warning, Hope flew from Deimos's lap, followed by her sister. They flew across the room and through the front door.

Deimos wasted no time following them as Ellie shrieked, "Girls, wait! Stop! Come back!"

Hermes overtook Deimos saying, "I'll catch up to them, cousin!"

Deimos couldn't breathe as he flew from Mount Kronos after his baby girls, unable to believe they'd taken off so quickly. To make matters worse, they seemed to be heading directly toward Mount Olympus.

"Stay put," Phobos said to Ellie. "I'll go."

"No way," Ellie said as her heart beat out of control. "I'm coming, too. Do you think we frightened them? Have they gone to hide?"

"I wish I knew," Phobos said. "Come on, then."

Artemis grabbed Phobos by the wrist. "Wait. Hades and Persephone are on their way with the chariot. Let's ride with them beneath the protection of the helm."

"I'm not waiting," Phobos said. "But, Ellie, you should go with them. You've got to be exhausted."

"I'm going with you," Ellie insisted, even though he was right about how tired she was.

"Faith and Hope are flying to Mount Olympus," Hecate said. "I've had a vision."

"Why?" Phobos groaned. "Why would they do this to us?"

Hecate shook her head and shrugged.

Hades appeared with the helm. "Who's coming with us?"

Everyone but Demeter climbed into Hades's chariot. It was a full wagon with Hades, Persephone, Hecate, and Artemis squeezed together in the front and Ellie, Phobos, Cupid, and Psyche in the back.

As they raced through the snowy sky, Phobos put an arm around Ellie and held her close, but she could barely feel him. All she could think about were her babies.

CHAPTER THIRTEEN

The Reckoning

Ellie held her breath as Hades and Persephone's chariot neared the gates of Mount Olympus.

Without a word from anyone, the gates opened, and standing there on the other side was Deimos. He couldn't see or hear them there, sitting silently in the chariot beneath the protection of the helm. Ellie wondered what he was doing.

Then, aloud, he said, "I pray to all the gods of the rebel alliance. If you can hear my prayer, please come to Mount Olympus. It's time for the reckoning."

It might be a trap, Hades prayed to those in the chariot. *He could be speaking under duress.*

One of us should go and see, Cupid said.

I'll go, Artemis said, and before anyone could object, she flew up from the chariot and revealed herself to Deimos.

Ellie watched as Deimos pointed toward the temple.

"What's going on, Deimos?" Artemis asked.

"Go and see for yourself," Deimos said with an air of defeat.

Ellie shuddered.

A few moments later, Artemis prayed, *The Fates have Faith and Hope and are at a stalemate with Zeus, who has the Garcia girls. I see no trap. Everyone's at a standstill. They're armed, so come with weapons ready.*

Hades slipped the helm onto Persephone's head and prayed, *One among us should remain invisible, as a precaution. Let Persephone go before the rest of us.*

Persephone left the vehicle and flew through the gates, unseen, exposing the chariot and its passengers to Deimos.

When the other gods of the rebellion conjured their weapons, Ellie did, too.

"Thank gods you're here," Deimos said. "They're waiting inside."

Phobos took Ellie by the hand and helped her to the gate, where Deimos waited.

"Are the babies okay?" Ellie asked Deimos.

Deimos lifted his palms. "They seem okay."

"Why did they come here?" Phobos asked.

"I think they were called by the Fates," he replied.

The three of them followed the others past the whale fountain and up the rainbow steps into the great hall of Zeus's temple, where they found Zeus and his loyalists gathered at the back of the room, near the thrones of Zeus and Hera.

Ellie searched frantically for her babies and found them with three old-looking women standing near the entrance to Hephaestus's forge. Hope and Faith were standing, too, with their wings tucked into their backs. Their hands were held by the old women.

"Faith! Hope!" Ellie cried, flying toward them.

One of the three old women lifted a bony finger. "You may stand with us, Ellie Beaufort, but Faith and Hope belong to us."

"Like hell, they do!" Ellie cried as she rushed to them and knelt at their feet. She curled her arms around her darlings' waists.

"What gall!" Aphrodite said from the other side of the room.

Ellie didn't know if the goddess was expressing criticism or admiration, but she didn't care.

"Those are the Fates," Phobos whispered in her ear. "Three sisters. The most powerful beings alive."

They didn't look very powerful. One wore a pink velvet pantsuit. Some of her gray hair was tied in a knot on the top of her head, while the rest of it fell to her shoulders. The sister in the middle was plump with short curly hair. She wore a bright blue shawl over a blue velvet dress. And the third, the one with black-rimmed spectacles, wore her white hair in a short bob with bangs. Her lavender jacket was also velvet, though her skirt was made of denim.

"I don't care who they are," Ellie shouted as tears of anger formed in her eyes. "I want my babies."

"They don't look like babies anymore," Deimos said.

He was right. They looked like two-year-old toddlers. They were no longer wearing the cute matching jumpers she'd dressed them in moments ago. They each wore white velvet gowns with a blue satin sash tied at the waist, and their hair had grown well past their ears.

"They'll always be our babies," Ellie said. And, to the Fates, she said, "Please, let them go."

"In due time," one of the Fates said in her old, crackly voice.

The members of the rebel alliance gathered near the entrance to the hall, on the opposite side of the temple to Zeus and his loyalists. Athena and Hephaestus stood with the loyalists until one of the Fates said, "Let's begin." Then Athena, followed by Hephaestus, crossed the room to stand beside Artemis and the other rebels.

Hermes also left the group of loyalists, but he remained in the middle of the temple, apparently not wishing to align himself with either side.

Zeus's eyebrows shot to the top of his forehead. "What's this?"

"Traitors!" Hera shouted.

"I knew it!" Ares cried.

That's when Ellie noticed Rose and Violet, held at the wrists by Hera, who stood angrily beside her husband. The girls were crying and trembling. Phobos and Deimos noticed them, too.

Phobos flew within five feet of the girls and said, "Hey, girlfriends."

"Help us, Phobos!" Rose said in a feeble voice.

"That's why I'm here," he said. "Don't worry. You'll be back home walking in pig poop before you know it."

Rose sucked in her lips but was too terrified to smile at Phobos's joke. Violet rubbed her eyes with her free hand and said, "Mimi. I want Mimi."

"I'll take you back to your Mimi and Papa soon," Phobos said.

"Can we get on with this?" Poseidon complained from where he stood on the other side of Zeus from Hera.

"Be careful what you wish for," one of the Fates said.

Ellie was nervous that Phobos remained near the loyalists, because of what happened in Hecate's vision. In the vision, Phobos fell, along with one of their daughters, with Hera and Zeus and other gods, when Mount Olympus crumbled.

Come stand by me, Ellie prayed to him from where she knelt beside their girls.

I'm bringing comfort to Rose and Violet, he said. *It's a nice change from bringing fear.*

But the vision, she said, though she knew she was being selfish. Rose and Violet needed him.

What vision?

No one had told Phobos about Hecate's vision.

One of the Fates, the one in the pink velvet pantsuit with part of her hair in a knot, left Hope and Faith with her sisters to cross to the center of the room.

"Lachesis, Atropos, and I have been waiting for this day for a long time with mixed feelings," she said. "As many of you know, we prefer to keep to ourselves and to play our games of chance in our modest chambers in the Underworld than to interact with others. Most gods and mortals only speak to us when they want to either know the future or to change it."

"That's true," the one in the blue velvet dress said.

"Like most of you, we didn't ask for our lot in the cosmos. We were born with it. As the spinner, it's my job to make sure that all beings serve a purpose and have varied experiences. And, while the three judges of the Underworld decide the punishment for the mortal souls that enter Hades, my sisters and I are tasked with judging the gods."

Ellie kissed the cheeks of her darling babies, trying to reassure them as everyone listened to what the Fate had to say.

"We've been waiting for Faith and Hope," the Fate said, which caused Ellie to gasp. "When Hephaestus made Pandora as per Zeus's instructions, hoping to counteract the power of fire bestowed on mortals by Prometheus, most of the ailments that plague humans escaped from Pandora's jar—all but hope. And for centuries now, humans have had to struggle to find hope. Many have failed. That lack of hope led to their loss of faith. Very few mortals even believe in our existence. And it's entirely the fault of *this* pantheon."

Zeus and Poseidon appeared indignant, but they said nothing.

The Fate continued: "As the spinner, I made it my mission to craft a time when Faith and Hope could be restored. I must say, it wasn't easy to bring these events together, was it, sisters?"

The other two Fates shook their heads.

"And I must also say how underappreciated I feel, but that's neither here nor there, so they say. This is what's important now, in this moment: this pantheon created humans. This pantheon has largely ignored the needs of humans. This pantheon was issued a final, crucial test to see if it was capable of serving humans above its own needs, and this pantheon failed."

Gasps filled the room.

"We merely reacted to the visions of doom you gave to me," Apollo said defensively.

"How can you fault us for trying to preserve our way of life?" Aphrodite said with tears in her eyes.

"Not all failed!" Hades insisted. "I and the gods who stand with me saved Ellie's life and protected her and her children."

"Oh, give it a break!" Ares shouted from across the room.

"This is *one* pantheon," the Fate said. "And this pantheon failed."

"But…" Artemis began.

"Those of you who fought to save Ellie Beaufort did so because it served your needs. Not a single god in this temple put his or her needs after those of the mortal, save Psyche."

Everyone turned to look at Psyche, who stood glancing back with wide eyes.

"Psyche is the only deity who acted for purely selfless reasons, but, unfortunately, even she will not be immune to our punishment."

"And what punishment is that?" Zeus cried, sounding half indignant and half afraid.

The Fate lifted her arms into the air.

Ellie screamed as the mountain shook and the pillars in the hall began to crumble. A crack ran through the marble floor of the temple between the rebel alliance and the loyalists, and before anyone had time to react, the side of the room with the loyalists plummeted into the earth, taking Phobos with them. In the next instant, Faith ripped herself from Ellie's embrace and flew to Phobos, down into the deep dark pit.

Deimos chased after Faith, dodging falling pillars and other rubble, but when he reached the pit, he found it blocked not only with rock but with wards that prevented him from seeing or traveling through to the other side.

Then as suddenly as it started, the shaking ceased. Deimos looked around at those who remained. Except for Faith and Phobos, the ones who had fallen had been loyalists. Hermes had managed to escape the pit, too.

Deimos turned to Clotho. "Where are they? What have you done with them?"

"Gaia has swallowed them," Clotho said.

"This can't be right," he said. "Swallowed?"

Clotho bowed her head. "I'm afraid so."

"No!" Ellie cried as she fell to her knees. "No, please! This isn't fair!"

Ellie buried her face against Hope's belly and wept.

It was a fate worse than death, and his brother and baby girl, along with his parents and other gods, were condemned to it.

And what of little Rose and Violet? If Gaia had swallowed them, they were dead.

The gods and goddesses of the rebel alliance stood, holding onto one another, in shock. They were speechless. As hard as they'd fought against Zeus and his loyalists, those gods were family, and now they were gone.

CHAPTER FOURTEEN

Aftermath

Deimos knelt beside Ellie but had no words for her. Ellie clung to Hope and wept.

Hope smoothed back Ellie's hair and comforted her.

Artemis shouted, "You Fates are hypocrites. Rose and Violet were innocent! Why couldn't you spare them? Or were they collateral damage?"

"They *were* spared," Atropos, the cutter said.

"What?" Deimos leapt to his feet.

"How?" Cupid asked.

"We instructed Hypnos to take them home and to put them to bed after erasing their memories," Lachesis, the measurer, said.

"Then why bring them here in the first place?" Psyche asked. "To torment them for nothing?"

"First of all, *we* didn't bring them," Atropos said.

"The loyalists did," Lachesis said.

"Gods and mortals have free will," Clotho pointed out. "The job of the Fates isn't to make decisions for people; it's to see the future and to orchestrate events that help them to better serve their purpose."

"Just because we know beforehand what people and gods will choose doesn't mean we *make* their choices," Atropos added.

"Second of all," Atropos said, "we needed the Garcia girls to summon Faith and Hope."

"But I thought *you* called them," Deimos said.

"No," Lachesis said.

"Little Rose prayed for Faith and Hope to come," Clotho explained.

Ellie and Deimos looked at their sweet darling Hope.

"Is that true?" Ellie asked her.

She put a finger in her mouth and nodded.

Hades stepped forward. "While this is all very interesting, where do we go from here? I mean, look at this place? And, by the way, Persephone, you can reveal yourself. No need to remain beneath the helm, my dear."

"Persephone isn't here," Lachesis said.

"Where is she?" Hecate asked.

"She fell with the others and was swallowed by Gaia," Atropos said.

"What?" Hades's face turned white.

"The helm, too," Clotho added.

"You're kidding," Hades said. "And it isn't funny."

"We're serious, Lord Hades," Lachesis said.

"But Persephone didn't deserve to fall with the others!" Hades raged around the room, causing more of the temple rubble to resettle. "Release her, this instant!"

"She *chose* it," Atropos said.

"Why would she *choose* such a Fate?" Hecate asked.

"Because like Psyche, she's one of the few among you capable of selfless acts," Clotho pointed out.

"How was that a selfless act?" Hades asked. "What good did getting swallowed by Gaia do for anyone else?"

"That's for us to know and for you to find out," the three Fates said in unison just before they disappeared.

Ellie sat at the round table in the throne room of the Underworld with the remaining Olympians as they discussed their next move. She held Hope on her lap, using her fingers to comb the little girl's curly red hair, which had grown to her shoulders. Deimos sat beside them with his elbows on the table and his head in his hands.

Athena and Hephaestus sat at the table on the other side of Deimos sharpening their blades. Cupid and Psyche sat in chairs across the room, apparently communicating telepathically with one another. Hades sat slumped on his throne, tugging at his beard, looking deep in thought. Artemis paced before the hearth. Hecate sat across from Ellie and Deimos with the ingredients of a spell laid out on the table before her. Hermes sat beside her, watching as she set herbs to fire and made incantations, apparently, to no avail.

Hypnos appeared beside Hecate. "What are you trying to do?"

"To communicate with Persephone," she said. "But it's not working."

An unfamiliar voice rang out from out of nowhere saying, "It's Amphitrite. Please grant me entrance. I have important news."

Hades snapped his fingers, and a beautiful goddess whom Ellie didn't recognize, appeared in the room before Hades and his throne.

"What news?" he asked.

"Word of Poseidon's imprisonment has reached the monsters of the sea," she said. "They're already taking measures to dominate Poseidon's realm. Without the trident, I can't stop them."

Her long, sun-bleached hair was twisted up in French rolls and fastened with a golden seashell comb and a headband made of crab pincers. The pincers clasped together at the center of her forehead, just above her turquoise eyes. Her blue gown was short and cinched at the waist with a jeweled belt resembling an eel.

Who's she? Ellie asked Deimos in prayer.

Amphitrite. Poseidon's wife.

Ellie had never imagined as a mortal that there were so many gods and goddesses. She could barely keep up with all their names.

"The sea is not my priority," Hades said to the new arrival. "I have no reinforcements to give you, no resources of any kind."

"And after they take over the sea?" Amphitrite asked. "What's to stop them from gaining control of the Underworld? From releasing the Titans? How hard would it be for Keto and Phorcys to turn their children, Cerberus and the Hydra, who are already here, against you? And, without the helm or the lightning bolt or the trident, how well can this pantheon defend itself?"

Ellie sighed. Being a goddess was nothing like she'd envisioned.

Deimos put an arm around her. *Don't be frightened. We'll figure out something.*

That didn't sound very convincing, but she made no reply.

Deimos listened as the other gods argued over what they should do about the uprising in the sea. Personally, he felt their priority should be finding a way to free the other Olympians from the belly of Gaia, but he understood Amphitrite's point.

He jumped up from the table and said, "We need to attack our problems on both fronts. Some of us need to help Amphitrite to defend the sea while the rest of us find a way to save our loved ones."

"We'll be weaker as a divided group," Artemis said.

"But time is of the essence," Hades argued. "As the only one here among us who has ever been swallowed by another deity, I can assure you that the longer we wait, the worse the trauma is."

"You've forgotten about me, Lord Hades," Athena said. "I lived in my father's belly for my entire childhood."

"So, you agree with me?" Hades asked.

"I agree with Deimos," Athena said. "We don't have a plan yet for how to free the others from Gaia, so those of us who are feeling restless should go and fight. I, for one, volunteer."

"I'll go, too," Hephaestus said.

Artemis raised her bow. "Then count me in."

"I'll go," Cupid said.

Psyche took his hand. "Stay."

"I'll go where I'm needed."

Seriously, brother? Deimos prayed.

Aloud, Cupid said, "If any of you have an idea for rescuing them, tell me now, and I'll do it; otherwise, I'll go and defend what's left of our reign."

"In that case," Hades said, "perhaps you should go, too, Hermes, since you're the fastest."

"Yes, my lord," Hermes said reluctantly. Then to Hecate, he said, "Don't give up. I know you can do it."

"The rest of you should have a plan ready by the time we get back," Artemis said, before she and the other volunteers left with Amphitrite.

"Who died and put her in charge?" Hades said with a scowl.

"Let's focus," Deimos said. "We don't have anything Gaia wants, right? We have no bargaining chip?"

"Right," Hades said.

"We have no way of invading?" Deimos asked. "There are no weak points of entry?"

"None that I know of," Hades said.

"This is a lost cause," Psyche wailed.

Deimos raked his hand through his hair, feeling frustrated.

Then Ellie asked, "How did Athena get free of her father, or you from yours, Lord Hades?"

Hecate emerged from her incantations over her candles and herbs to say, "Athena sprang from Zeus's head after Hephaestus hit him with a cleaver."

"That was a bold move," Ellie said.

"Zeus asked him to do it, because he had a horrible headache for eons," Hades said.

"And what about you, Lord Hades?" Ellie asked. "How did you escape?"

"Zeus tricked our father into swallowing an herb that made him vomit," Hades said.

"Couldn't we give Gaia an herb?" Ellie asked.

Hecate shook her head. "Herbs won't work on her. Anything that grows from the earth will not poison her."

"So, we need something synthetic," Ellie said. "An unnatural poison."

"It's not as simple as that," Hades said. "Gaia can absorb almost anything—gasoline, acid, and just about any synthetic substance you can think of."

"What about explosives?" Ellie said.

Deimos lifted his brows. "That's an idea. We could blow up the earth and set the others free."

Hades picked his beard. "It's a dangerous proposition. Anything that would blow up Gaia would cause destruction to the other gods, too. We'd have to rescue decapitated heads and limbs to preserve their bodies. If Gaia were to recover before we'd retrieved every ounce of flesh of our fellow Olympians, we'd risk leaving some behind, or worse, finding ourselves trapped right along with them."

"I'm willing to take that risk," Deimos said. "If there's no other way."

"Me, too," Ellie said.

"Count me in," Hecate said.

"And me as well," said Psyche.

"Then it sounds as if we have a plan," Hades said. "Let's gather what we need for the explosives and wait for the others to return. We'll need all hands on deck to carry out this mission."

Ellie carried her sleeping daughter to the guest chamber in the Underworld and lay down in the bed beside her. Not having rested since giving birth, Ellie felt she could finally allow herself to close her eyes, now that there was a plan in place.

The moment she did, the only thing she could think of was how frightened Faith must be in the belly of Gaia. With all her heart, she wished that Faith and Phobos were comforting one another and that they hadn't given up hope.

She still hadn't fallen asleep about a half hour later when Deimos came to check on her. She looked up at him as he stood over her and combed her hair from her eyes.

Telepathically, so as not to wake the sleeping Hope, Deimos prayed, *How are you holding up?*

As well as can be expected.

You know, we wouldn't have a plan if it weren't for you. You truly showed your power today as the goddess of lost causes. I have a feeling you'll be helping mortals and gods alike in unexpected ways.

I can't even think about that right now.

I know.

I hear the prayers of people constantly. I know I should do something. But all I can think about is Faith and Phobos. We have to help them, Deimos. We have to.

Ellie couldn't stop the new round of tears that spilled from her eyes. She was so tired of crying.

Deimos knelt on the floor beside the bed and gently wiped her tears with his thumbs.

I wish I could say that I was sorry that the gods involved you in this mess, he prayed. *But you know why I can't. I have been alive for centuries, and in less than a year, you have made my life.*

She squeezed his hand. *My sweet Deimos.*

In many ways, I didn't start living until I met you.

Let's hope it doesn't end with us all trapped inside of Gaia.

As long as we're together, I can stand just about anything.

As tired as she was, she carefully lifted herself from the bed and met him in the air, away from their sleeping child. She relished the feeling of being in his arms. He held her close, in a tight embrace, and rocked her in the air.

Then he surprised her by singing:

You are the light of my life. You give me Faith and Hope to endure hard times.

You're the one I breathe for, the one for whom my heart pines.
You make the darkness bright and the wrongs all right.
Although I laughed before I met you, I never knew real happiness.
And though I cried, the thought of losing you teaches me true sadness.
You are the light of my life, my love, my darling, my dear, sweet wife.

Ellie had never heard him sing before and was amazed by his beautiful voice. More tears filled her eyes as she wrapped her arms tightly around his neck. Then he cupped her cheeks and gently pressed his lips to hers. Peace and desire washed over her as she accepted his kisses. His love for her gave her the strength she needed to exist in that moment.

CHAPTER FIFTEEN

A New Way

Deimos woke up beside Ellie and, noticing that she was still asleep between him and their sleeping daughter, carefully extricated himself from her arms, changed clothes, and flew to the throne room, hoping for an update on the war with the sea monsters. Instead, he found Hecate waiting for him.

"I've had an idea," she said. "And since the others aren't back from the sea, I was hoping you'd help me."

"Anything, Hecate. Just tell me what you need me to do."

A few minutes later, Deimos flew with Hecate in Hades's chariot across the sky over the Ionian Sea toward Circe's Island. Memories from the hollowed-out tree made him smile.

They parked the chariot in the twisted trees on the edge of the clearing where Circe's angular lair, made of stone and glass, was situated at the bottom of a hill. Smoke ascended in ribbons from the chimney—a sign that the witch was home.

"One never knows Circe's mood from one moment to the next," Hecate warned as they carefully made their way down the hill.

"Hopefully marriage agrees with her," Deimos said.

"Even when she's happy, she rarely does something for nothing. We need to be prepared to make a trade."

"Any ideas?"

"No. But maybe something will come to mind."

Deimos inwardly groaned, wishing they had a better plan.

Three wolves and three mountain lions paced the perimeter of the house. As Deimos and Hecate approached, two of the wild dogs bounded toward them.

"Keep walking," Hecate said. "The dogs will only bite if they smell fear."

Deimos braced himself as the wolves reached him and was delighted when they licked his hand.

"Good dogs," he said, patting their heads.

Circe opened her door before they knocked.

"What a surprise," she said in her crackly, witchy voice.

"We need your help," Hecate said.

Circe said, "Tsk, tsk, tsk. Of course, you do. That's the only reason anyone comes to see me. Come inside, please, and have a seat at my table. I was just about to have some breakfast."

Deimos followed Hecate inside. The kitchen was filled with surprisingly pleasing aromas.

"Would you like some eggs and sausage?" Circe asked.

"That sounds delicious," Deimos said.

"None for me, thanks," Hecate said.

Circe made plates for her and Deimos and brought them to the table, along with goblets of juice for each of them, including Hecate.

Deimos took a bite of the sausage. "Delicious. Thank you."

"Where's James?" Hecate asked. "Have the two of you been enjoying married life?"

Circe frowned and rolled her eyes. "He was the most selfish man I've ever known, and that's saying something. He loved me, yes, but he loved himself more. In bed, he cared less about pleasing me than himself. And at night, when the blood runs down my walls, he refused to leave the house to sleep with me in my hollowed-out tree. He claimed there was no blood on the walls. The man was as blind as he was selfish."

"But Cupid shot you in the heart," Deimos said. "Don't you still love James? Aren't you bound to him?"

"You're speaking to a witch who practices black magic. You don't think I have a potion for curing love?"

"So, where is he?" Deimos asked.

"I turned him into a pig and ate him," Circe said. "In fact, these sausages are the last of him."

Deimos spit out the food in his mouth and wiped his face with a napkin.

"I thought you said it was delicious," Circe said.

Deimos pushed the plate away from him. "I'm suddenly not very hungry."

"What's this favor you wish to ask of me, Hecate?"

Deimos and Hecate explained to Circe what had happened to the other Olympians—the ones swallowed by Gaia.

"Do you have a potion that would make Gaia sleep long enough for us to recover all the bodies of our friends after the explosions?" Hecate asked.

"I have something better," Circe said.

Deimos's curiosity was piqued.

"There's a way to open Gaia without explosives," Circe said. "The spell is powerful. It requires the god of the sun, the moon, the sky, and the sea."

"We could ask Helios, Selene, and Amphitrite," Deimos began, "but what sky god? Zeus is obviously unavailable."

"Aether," Hecate said. "But no one has seen him for centuries."

"I have a hair from his head," Circe said. "We can easily find him."

"Why do you have one of his hairs?" Deimos asked.

"I have a hair from everyone's head," Circe said. "You never know when one might come in handy."

Deimos lifted his brows. He hoped she never used one of his.

"Tell me about the spell, Circe," Hecate said. "What's involved? How does it work?"

"The sun, moon, sky, and sea join hands," Circe said. "I have a special recipe that I will pour onto the earth. Then I'll recite an incantation that will cause the winds to blow across the earth in a raging system of hurricanes, the sea to rise in mighty tidal waves, and the earth to quake so violently, that Gaia will crack apart, freeing the other gods."

"Just like that?" Deimos asked. "The other gods can slip away, unharmed? No casualties?"

"I wouldn't say *no casualties*," Circe said. "The winds, waves, and earthquakes are likely to cause a lot of damage, killing hundreds—if not thousands—of people and animals."

Deimos frowned. "Oh."

Deimos considered the pros and cons and decided that he had to do whatever it took to save his child, brother, and parents.

"We can't tell Ellie, or she will find a way to talk us out of it," he said. "The same is true for Psyche."

"They'll find out about the loss of life soon after," Hecate pointed out.

"*After* being the important word," Deimos said. "It's better to ask forgiveness than permission. By then, my daughter, brother, and parents will be safe."

"But Ellie may never forgive you," Hecate said.

"I'll have plenty of time to win back her heart," Deimos said. "Eventually, she'll see that we did what we had to do to save our loved ones."

"We'll have to discuss this with the others," Hecate said.

"Of course," Circe said.

"Is there something you want in return?" Hecate asked the witch.

"Another match from Cupid—a better match."

"I don't believe I can make a promise to you on the behalf of another," Hecate said.

"So long as you promise to make a case to Cupid for me, I'm satisfied."

"That I can do," Hecate said. "We'll let you know our answer soon."

In the chariot on the return trip to the Underworld, Deimos said, "This is a no brainer. I'm sad that lives will be lost, but thousands of people die every day *already*."

"Not by our hands."

"No."

"We need to think this through, Deimos. We can't make a rash decision based on emotion."

"I'll find a way to distract Ellie and Psyche while you present the idea to the others."

Ellie was in the throne room of the Underworld eating at the round table with Hope, Deimos, Cupid, and Psyche, while Hades sat slumped on his throne and Hecate tirelessly worked on her spells. The rice and vegetables looked and smelled delicious, but Ellie's appetite was gone, because she was too worried about Faith and Phobos.

Three days had gone by since the others had left to fight in the sea. Cupid had prayed with an update that things were looking grim and that all but Amphitrite would be returning soon for a rest.

When she noticed that Hope wasn't eating, either, she said, "Aren't you hungry, Hope?"

The little girl shook her head.

"But you need food to grow," Ellie said, even though her daughter was growing too fast already Her mother had taught her that food was important, so she wanted to teach her children the same. "Can you take a bite, for me?"

"You," Hope said.

Ellie nodded and took a bite of the rice. It stimulated her appetite, so she ate more. Hope ate some, too.

They hadn't yet finished their meal when the battle-worn warriors returned from the sea, wet and exhausted.

"What's the status?" Hades asked as he jumped to his feet.

Hermes shook his head. "The monsters are gaining ground in all the major seas."

"We need more fighters," Artemis said. "Phorcys and Keto are out of control."

Deimos glanced at Hecate before turning to Ellie and Psyche. "Why don't the three of us take Hope to visit the Garcias? We can make sure Danny and Christina have no memory of the incident, and that they're all doing well."

"That's a great idea," Ellie said.

"You go on without me," Psyche said. "Cupid looks like he could use some tender loving care after all that fighting."

"But I think they'd be happy to see you, too, Psyche," Deimos said. "Don't you?"

"I doubt it, to tell you the truth. I wasn't the happiest and most efficient ranch hand they'd ever met."

Cupid joined them at the table and had overheard Psyche. "That's an understatement."

Psyche laughed. "Besides, I was under the impression that we were going to go forward with our plan to free the others as soon as possible."

"Indeed," Hades said from where he stood before his throne. "Warriors rest and eat, and then let's discuss how to bring the others back from the belly of Gaia."

Deimos leaned over the table and said, "Why don't we pop over to west Texas—you, me and Psyche—while the others are resting? We can be back in no time."

"We've been waiting on the warriors to return for days," Psyche said. "Why didn't you propose this idea yesterday, or the day before, or the day before that? Are you trying to get us to go for some other reason?"

Ellie narrowed her eyes at Deimos. "Think carefully before you answer."

Deimos sighed before turning to Hecate. "This isn't going to work."

"I could have told you that and saved you the trouble," she said.

"Why didn't you?" he asked.

"You wouldn't have believed me."

"See that in a vision?" Deimos asked with a touch if irritation in his tone.

"What's going on, Deimos?" Cupid asked.

"Hecate and I have found another way to save the others, but Ellie and Psyche aren't going to like it."

"No one's going to *like* it," Hecate said. "But some may, nevertheless, support it."

Ellie frowned. Had Deimos really hoped to deceive her?

"Don't be mad, Ellie," Deimos said.

She wasn't sure what to say to that, so she said nothing.

"What's this about?" Hades asked from his throne. "Deimos and Hecate have found another way, and I haven't heard about it yet?"

"We were waiting on the others, Lord Hades," Deimos said.

"Spit it out," Artemis said. "We can rest when the others are free."

Hecate stood up and told them about a visit she and Deimos had made to see Circe.

When was this? Ellie prayed to Deimos.

A few days ago, he replied.

Ellie fumed. Didn't her husband respect her enough to tell her?

"Essentially, we need sun, moon, sea, and sky to join hands during an incantation, as a potion is poured onto Gaia," Hecate was saying.

"Helios, Selene, Amphitrite, and…?" Hephaestus asked.

Athena turned to Hecate. "Aether?"

Hecate nodded.

Who's that? Ellie asked Deimos.

The god of the upper sky. He keeps to himself.

"No one has seen or heard from him in centuries," Hades pointed out.

"Circe has a way," Deimos said. "Apparently, she collects hairs for just that purpose."

"What are you not telling us?" Hades asked. "This sounds too easy, and, as I always say, everything comes with a price."

"Indeed, Lord Hades," Hecate said. "She's asked me to convince Cupid to give her another match. The first one didn't work out so well. She turned James Lorenzo into a pig and ate him."

Ellie covered her mouth in shock. Her biological father was dead? And Deimos didn't tell her?

"She can't enforce that," Artemis said. "You don't control Cupid."

"Circe knows as much," Hecate said. "But the price is worse than that, I'm afraid. Far worse. Circe practices black magic, and it always comes with a terrible price. That's why she's lost her mind. That's why she sees blood on her walls at night."

"And what's the price?" Hades asked.

Hecate glanced at Deimos, who said, "The spell will cause the winds to blow as hurricanes, the sea to rise in tidal waves, and the earth to violently quake. Although it will crack Gaia open and free the others, unscathed, it will likely kill thousands of humans and animals."

Ellie sought Deimos's eyes. *This was why you didn't tell me?*

He nodded.

You're willing to pay the price of all those lives to save Faith and Phobos?

Again, he nodded.

The other gods were silent. Ellie was, too.

CHAPTER SIXTEEN

Circe's Spell

L et's take twenty-four hours to think this through," Hades said after Hecate and Deimos had told him the plan. "That will give Hecate time to perform the location spell and to find Aether."

Ellie gnawed on her bottom lip, feeling nauseated. She pushed her plate away and said, "I need to lie down and think."

"Can I go explore the bat cave with Hypnos?" Hope asked.

"There's a bat cave?" Ellie asked.

Hope nodded as Hypnos appeared beside her.

"I can keep an eye on her, if you'd like," Hip offered. "You could use the rest. You haven't slept for more than a few hours since those three weeks in the asphodel."

"That would be great, Hip," Deimos said. "She hasn't gotten enough rest since giving birth."

"Don't leave her alone for a second," Ellie said to Hip. Then, turning to Hope, she said, "Don't fly off without Hypnos, okay?"

Hope nodded and then, with a smile on her face, she disappeared with the god of sleep.

Deimos took Ellie by the hand, and together they left the throne room and went, down the hall, to the guest chamber.

They climbed into bed and held one another and were quiet for several minutes before Ellie said, "I can't believe you were going to lie to me."

"You would have discovered the truth, soon enough."

"I wish you'd trusted me."

Deimos smoothed her hair from her eyes. "I know you well enough to know you wouldn't want to go through with it, not if thousands of lives would be lost."

"You're wrong."

Deimos lifted her chin and met her eyes with his. "Seriously?"

"So, I guess you don't know me as well as you thought."

"Don't be angry with me, Ellie. I can't stand it."

She sighed. "And when were you going to tell me that James Lorenzo was dead?"

"I thought it would be too much to take right now. But I was going to tell you."

"I'm stronger than you think."

He studied her face. "I know you're strong." He closed his eyes and rolled onto his back. "Oh, Ellie. I know you're strong, I'm the one who's weak. I feel so desperate and helpless. I can't fucking stand it."

He was relieved when she laid her cheek on his chest and circled his waist with her slender arm. He took a deep breath and sighed.

"Tell me it's the right thing to do," Ellie said.

"It's definitely not the right thing to do, Ellie. But I think we should do it anyway."

Ellie buried her face against Deimos's chest, ashamed of herself. Was she really willing to kill thousands of people and animals to save Faith and Phobos from Gaia's belly? What if her mother and Dominique and Jonivan were hurt in the winds, waves, and earthquakes—or killed, even? What about Shaylynn and her family? What about Ellie's other teammates, classmates, teachers, friends? Were their lives worth less than her happiness?

Was it possible that Faith and Phobos could find some kind of life in the belly of Gaia? Maybe it was wrong to assume they were suffering. If she could imagine them happy together, maybe she could go on. She and Deimos could raise Hope together and make a life without Faith and Phobos. Mortals did it all the time when they lost their loved ones.

Ellie shuddered against Deimos. The difference was that mortals could imagine their loved ones at peace. From what the other gods had said, there wasn't any peace to be had in the belly of another deity.

"My sweet Ellie," Deimos said stroking her hair. "I don't know how I'd make it through all of this without you."

Ellie didn't say it, but it made her imagine Phobos wondering how he could make it through eternity without her. "We've got to get them out of there."

"I know. Oh, Ellie. I know."

She lifted her face and kissed him. "We have no choice, Deimos. We do, but we don't. Mortals can find peace in the Fields of Elysium. But Faith and Phobos…"

"I know." He pulled her tightly against him.

Ellie clung to him, needing to feel every inch of him beneath her. Like Deimos, she felt desperate and helpless and nearly dead with despair. But she didn't want to feel dead. She wanted to feel alive and powerful and in control. She pressed her lips hard against his mouth. He hungrily returned her kisses.

Then he whipped her around, onto her back, and ripped off her clothes. With a feverish passion, he squeezed breasts, bit her lips, and thrust inside her, hard and angry. She moaned with pleasure and pressed back, just as hard against him. They rammed their bodies against one another, hurting and pleasuring at once until at last, they climaxed.

Deimos collapsed on the bed beside her.

Ellie closed her eyes, catching her breath. Deimos reached across the bed and held her hand. They lay there, holding hands without speaking until, at some point, Ellie fell asleep.

Deimos stood with Ellie and Hope on the rubble that had once been the temple of Mount Olympus, along with the other members of the rebel alliance—save Hecate and Hermes, who had gone to persuade Aether to come.

They were all counting on Hermes's powers of persuasion.

The sun used to always shine on Mount Olympus, but it did so no more. The winds railed against the mountain beneath a dark sky with no moon, blowing the hair and clothes of all present in every direction. Clutching the hands of her parents, Hope stood between Ellie and Deimos in the outer circle formed by the rebels. Helios, Selene, and Amphitrite formed the inner circle.

I really hope we're doing the right thing, Ellie prayed to Deimos for the hundredth time.

I hope so, too, he said.

I'm so afraid for my family.

And the Garcia family, I know.

And my softball mates.

And every person you've ever known.

And every person I haven't known.

I know, Ellie.

I'm such a hypocrite. I'm doing the very opposite of my purpose. I'm forcing people into a lost cause.

Have you changed your mind, then? You don't want to do this?

I want Faith. I want Phobos. The people who die tonight will find peace. But if we don't do this, Faith and Phobos will suffer with the other gods for all eternity.

Then we're still on the same page?

It's too risky to go with the plan of blowing them up, right?

Right. We may not recover all the parts. It was a good plan when there was no other option.

Ellie took a deep breath and nodded. *We're on the same page.*

Deimos's heart felt like it was breaking in two as he watched Ellie struggle with what they were about to do. He understood how she felt. All the gods present had expressed the same hesitations and misgivings. They stood together that night in solemn silence.

Psyche was the only among them who had unequivocally opposed the plan of using Circe's spell, but even she stood with them, resigned. She had finally admitted that if Cupid had been swallowed, her opinion might be different.

Everyone else had a brother, a spouse, a parent, a child, or a sibling—someone that they could not bear to live without. They'd justified carrying out the spell by arguing that eternity was a long time. The suffering of mortals was but a moment compared to the eternal lives of the gods.

But Deimos still felt uneasy. He sensed they all did. None expressed confidence as they stood and waited. He wondered if some were hoping that Hermes and Hecate would fail in their mission. Without Aether, the spell couldn't be done.

Ellie pressed her face against Deimos's neck, overwhelmed with guilt and fear. And when Hecate and Hermes arrived with the god whom she presumed was Aether, Ellie shuddered. Were they really going to go through with this?

The thought of never seeing Faith or Phobos again made her anxious for the gods to begin the spell; but the nausea in the pit of her stomach, the erect hairs on the back of her neck, and the pain gripping and twisting her heart made her want to cry out against the deed.

The gods were silent as Hecate stood in the center of the inner circle with a vial of potion from Circe. Helios, Selene, Amphitrite, and Aether joined hands as Hecate said:

Sun, Moon, Sea, and Sky,

To you with urgent need we cry.

"Wait!" Hades shouted.

Everyone turned to stare at the lord of darkness.

He marched to the center of the inner circle to stand beside Hecate. He took the vial from her and held it high in the air.

"It kills me to make this argument. As you all know, the love of my life suffers along with the others swallowed by Gaia. But we can't do this. I'm responsible for the souls of the dead. I have never killed an innocent mortal—not to mention thousands—and I can't, however badly I want my wife—do it today."

He made the vial from Circe disappear into thin air.

Ellie, along with the other gods, gasped.

"We'll find another way," Hades said. "We made the argument to use the spell because eternity is a long time, but that's the very reason *not* to use the spell. We have time. We have time to find a better way that won't result in the loss of innocent lives."

Suddenly, the earth began to shake. Ellie took Hope into her arms and, along with the other gods, lifted from the ground and watched with astonishment as the mountain cracked in half, as it had on the day of the reckoning. Then, like a swarm of bees, the fallen gods flew out of the earth and into the air.

Ellie screamed with joy when Faith and Phobos found her and Deimos and Hope. She embraced them with all her might, flabbergasted by their sudden appearance. Was it real? Was this really happening? The other gods, too, shouted with glee as they were reunited with loved ones. Deimos even hugged Ares and Aphrodite, as though they hadn't put their sons through hell.

Once all the gods were free of the earth, the mountain shook again as the crack resealed itself. Then the marble floor of the great hall was restored piece by piece. Columns resurrected from the rubble—thrones, too. With a flash of light and a swirl of stars, the temple was rebuilt on Mount Olympus, along with the blue sky above.

The gods gathered in the main hall of the temple, holding one another with surprise, relief, and gratitude, when suddenly the Fates appeared hovering above them. The gods backed away from the center of the room, toward the perimeter to make way as the Fates descended.

Some of the gods found their thrones and sat down. Then the Fates landed on the marble floor in the middle of them.

Ellie stood between Phobos and Deimos, who each held one of their girls. She blinked and pinched herself, worried that Hypnos had given her a dream.

"Figments," she whispered to Phobos and Faith. "I command you to show yourself."

When they smiled back at her without turning into eel-like creatures, she began to accept the fact that her family had been restored.

Deimos couldn't stop kissing Faith's cherub cheeks and clapping his brother, Phobos, on the back. He'd begun to believe that he'd never see them again and was overwhelmed with relief and joy.

When the Fates landed in the middle of the great hall of Mount Olympus, the chatter among the gods ended and all stood silently waiting for the Fates to say whatever it was they had come to say.

"Congratulations to you all," Clotho, the spinner, said as she clasped her hands together. "You have survived the reckoning."

"We know you have questions," Atropos said. "And we are prepared to answer them."

"No need to ask," Lachesis said. "We already know what they are."

"The test for the gods was two-fold," Clotho said. "One involved the life of Ellie Beaufort and her apparent threat to your pantheon."

"The rebel alliance chose the right side," Lachesis said, "but it wasn't clear what motivated them."

Atropos pushed her spectacles further up on her nose. "So, we forced the rebels to choose between the lives of thousands of mortals and the freedom of their loved ones."

"In one spectacular moment," Lachesis began, "Hades passed the test, as we knew he would."

"If you knew he would," Zeus said, "why make us endure the reckoning in the first place?"

"We saw the choices you would make, it's true," Clotho said. "But you still needed to make them."

"That's messed up," Ares complained.

Deimos didn't care about the why or the how; he only cared that he and his family were together again. He couldn't wait to go home, to start their lives.

"We have one more sentence to hand out before you go," Atropos said. "Zeus and the loyalists who joined him are hereby condemned to be stripped of their powers for one month and to work on the west Texas ranch for the Garcias."

"What?" Hera cried.

"Is this a joke?" Apollo demanded.

Deimos's mouth dropped open. Ellie's smile cracked her face in half. Phobos busted out with laughter.

"In addition to shoveling manure, you'll be doing home repairs," Clotho added. "So be sure to take along some extra tools and paint brushes."

"We just spent three days in the belly of Gaia!" Poseidon bellowed. "Isn't that punishment enough?"

"Watch your tone," Lachesis said with her hands on her hips.

"If you wish to reject our sentence, you may, Poseidon," Atropos said, "but only if you're willing to return our trident."

"*Your* trident?" he raged.

"I think that means he'll serve," Atropos said.

Phobos put one arm around Deimos and the other around Ellie and busted out laughing again.

CHAPTER SEVENTEEN

Homecoming

This high altitude is making me feel sick," Aphrodite complained as Deimos and Phobos drove a chariot full of loyalists, stripped of their powers, toward the Garcia ranch on a beautiful day in mid-February.

"It's the motion that bothers *me*," Ares said. "I think I'm going to throw up."

"What big babies," Deimos said with a laugh.

Deimos couldn't wait to see how they fared in the pig pen.

Cupid and Psyche followed in a second chariot with another group of the condemned, and Ellie and Artemis brought up the rear with the last load. Deimos could hear similar complaints coming from the other carloads of loyalists.

Poseidon was saying to Cupid, "Can't you slow down? I think I'm getting windburn."

And Apollo said to Artemis, "Wipe that smug grin off your face, sister."

The drivers brought their chariots to a halt just outside the south fence before leading the gods, on foot, up the road, past the pond, and toward the front porch, where the Garcias were waiting. Each god carried a bag of clothing and toiletries and a bag of groceries to help with all the extra mouths to feed. Zeus and Ares also carried tents that would be pitched near the shack for the overflow housing.

Artemis led the way and was the first to reach the Garcias.

Danny shook her hand and said, "When you called and said you were bringing more help, I didn't know you meant an army."

Phobos said, telepathically to Deimos, *Little does he know it* is *an army.*

Rose and Violet ran up to hug Phobos and Deimos, but fear and panic made them stop a few feet away.

"It's okay, girlfriends," Phobos said. "You're right to stay back. Deimos stinks, and I've got a cold."

The girls laughed.

"You're funny, Phobos," Rose said.

"Don't say that," Deimos warned. "It'll go to his head."

Ellie, who had been hugging Jaquelyn and catching up with her, now turned to embrace the little girls.

"Where'd you go?" Rose asked her. "We missed you."

"Now, now," Christina said to Rose. "Don't be a nosey Rosie."

"I missed you, too," Ellie said. "What do you think about the help we brought?"

"It's a lot of people!" Violet said in her little voice.

Deimos and Phobos laughed.

"Hopefully they'll be more help than pains in the you-know-what," Phobos said.

"In the butt?" Rose asked.

"Rosie!" Christina scolded.

"Don't blame her," Deimos said. "That's exactly what Phobos meant."

The Australian shepherds, Julio and Iglesias, ran up to greet them. Ellie knelt on the gravel path and loved on each one. Mo, the indoor dog, soon followed.

"Where's Deimos the cat?" Phobos asked Jaquelyn.

"Oh, he's around here somewhere. You know how he likes to do his own thing."

"He takes after his namesake," Deimos said with a laugh.

"In more ways than one," Phobos said. "He cleans himself with his tongue, too."

"Gross!" the little girls said, giggling.

Cupid and Psyche, who were previously talking with Danny, came over to say their hellos.

"I'm sorry I can't stay," Psyche said.

Phobos threw his head back and guffawed. "You know that's a load of poop, don't you, girls?"

Rose and Violet giggled again.

"We better let them get settled in," Artemis said to Deimos and the other drivers.

"We'll be back in a month," Deimos said to the other gods. "See you then!"

"Hey, Mother!" Phobos called out to Aphrodite, who was watching Ares pitch their tent on the edge of the driveway. "Our father may not be much good to you in the pig pen. We hear he's a real BOAR! Bwhahahaha!"

"Goodbye!" Ellie and Cupid shouted as they walked toward the south fence.

"Bye!" Christina and the girls shouted as they waved.

"How long do you think our mother will last?" Deimos asked Phobos, as they took off in their father's chariot.

"Not even a day," Phobos said. "And I can't wait to see her when she falls in all that horse shit."

"How do you know she will?" Deimos asked.

"I asked to borrow the helm to make sure of it, bro'."

Deimos laughed and laughed all the way back to Mount Olympus.

As much as Ellie enjoyed seeing the Garcias again, she was glad to return to Mount Olympus, to Aphrodite's luxurious empty rooms, where Faith and Hope were waiting.

She and Phobos and Deimos spent the next few days teaching their girls about some of the basic godly powers and rules. They showed them how to god-travel and explained why it was faster but not as safe as flight and chariot-travel. They practiced god-traveling all over the world. They went to Egypt to see the great pyramids, to Turkey to see the first temple built for Artemis in Ephesus, to Delphi to see Apollo's oracle, to Italy to see the leaning tower of Pisa, and to Rome to see the coliseum.

After all that god-travel, Phobos and Deimos taught the girls how to drive a chariot all the way to New York, where they saw the Niagara Falls. From there, they journeyed north, to Mont Forel, to see Selene's cave and then further east, to the coast of Baffin Bay, to park awhile and watch the Northern Lights.

From there, Phobos and Deimos told the girls to drive the chariot back toward Greece, to the Aegean Sea, down to the very bottom of the ocean, where they payed a visit to Poseidon's Palace. Amphitrite wasn't at home, because she'd taken the trident and an army of gods to put all the sea monsters back in their places, but other merfolk were there to give them the tour.

Then they took the chariot up from the sea, into the sky, and down through the narrow chasm leading to the Underworld, where they sought permission from Hades to have a tour. Hades instructed Charon to allow the family onto his raft, and the old god took them past the giant three-headed dog to see the gorgeous Fields of Elysium, the fragrant Fields of Asphodel, and the frightful Tartarus, before letting them off to tour inside the Palace of Hades and Persephone.

And Hope insisted on showing them the bat cave.

They returned to Mount Olympus to park the chariot and unbridle the horses before they god-traveled to Psyche and Cupid's palace, where they'd been invited to join their hosts in the living room to sit before the fireplace. Cupid shot an arrow to reveal the loyalists working on the Garcia Ranch. Ellie, Phobos, Deimos, and their girls ate popcorn with Cupid and Psyche and laughed at the misfortune of gods who had been unkind. It made their hearts a little more open to the possibility of for-giveness.

After a few more weeks of tours and instruction with the girls, Ellie wanted to do one more thing before she went to work as the goddess of lost causes. She wanted to take her immortal family to visit her mother, sister, and Jonivan, and she wanted to tell her mortal family the truth without wiping their memories. In fact, she wanted to restore their memories from Cupid's castle and Demeter's winter cabin.

She waited for a Saturday, when she knew her mother, sister, and nephew would be home. Deimos and Phobos helped her to feed the girls something from Hestia's kitchen before they took Ares's chariot across the sky to her mother's house in the Lower Ninth Ward of New Orleans.

"We can't show up in this chariot," Ellie said, as they descended to-ward the neighborhood. "Let's park it over there. I've got an idea."

They landed Ares's chariot and horses behind an old industrial build-ing. Then, in invisibility mode, Ellie led her husbands and children from the chariot across town to the limousine rental, where she and her high school friends once rented a limo to take them to prom.

"What are we doing here?" Phobos asked.

"I'm buying my mama a limo and hiring her a full-time driver," Ellie explained.

"You do know that money can't buy happiness," Deimos warned.

Phobos cocked his head to the side. "Nor can poverty, bro'."

Once the papers were signed and the money paid, Ellie asked their driver to take them to see a real estate agent in the French Quarter.

On the way, Ellie cracked open cans of soda for the girls to taste.

"I like the fizziness," Faith said.

"It's definitely not milk," Hope said, as though she hadn't yet formed an opinion. "But I do like car travel. It's fun."

"Me, too," Faith said.

"That's because we're in a limousine," Ellie said with a laugh. "I doubt you'd like it so much in a cramped compact car during rush hour traffic."

"I have no idea what you're saying," Hope said.

"You'll catch on," Deimos said.

"Can we at least take the girls for beignets while we're here?" Phobos asked.

Ellie flapped her hand in the air. "You're such a tourist, Phobos!"

"What are beignets?" Hope asked.

"Fried dough rolled in powdered sugar," Deimos said.

"Very healthy," Phobos added.

"Why don't you two take the girls for beignets while I buy my mama and sister a mansion in the French Quarter?" Ellie suggested.

"Just an average day in the life of a goddess," Phobos teased.

"Oh, come on, Phobos," Deimos said. "You know that's only true when gods are battling gods…"

"And the monsters are rising in the seas," Hope added.

"And Mount Olympus is crumbling," Faith said.

"Now look, Deimos," Phobos complained. "You're rubbing off on Hope and Faith. If *they* can't be optimistic about an average day in the life of a goddess, who can?"

Deimos sat at the table at Café du Monde with Phobos and their daughters enjoying beignets when he heard a prayer from Hecate about Dominique's biological father.

He mentioned it to Phobos. "The guy's name is Benny Munos. He doesn't live far from here. Do you mind if we check him out before I mention this to Ellie?"

"Why is this so important to you?" Phobos asked. "Ellie hasn't brought it up, has she?"

Deimos shook his head. "I guess I'm angry about my Amazonian daughter—a daughter that I may never get to meet. Maybe Benny

Munos never knew about Dominique. Or maybe there's an explanation for his absence in her life. Fathers have rights, too, you know."

With the address from Hecate in hand, the fathers and daughters left the café, made themselves invisible to mortals, and flew along the Mississippi River, following a tributary toward Claiborne Avenue Bridge where they found, not a private residence, but a dog rescue shelter.

The four gods flew around the facility, spying on the mortals, careful not to alert the dogs, who could often sense gods.

"Look how adorable that puppy is!" Faith said to her sister, where they hovered high in the air.

"Oh, Dads, can we have one?" Hope asked. "They're all so cute and in need of love."

Phobos rolled his eyes. "What were we thinking, bringing them here, Deimos?"

"I wasn't thinking."

"For once, you're right. We can't take a dog back with us, can we?" Phobos looked as if he'd already yielded.

"*Two* dogs!" Faith said.

Hope nodded eagerly. "One for each of us."

Deimos lifted his hands in the air. "Wait a minute. Not so fast."

"Dad!" Faith said pointing. "I heard that girl call that man *Benny*. Do you think that's Benny Munos?"

"Let's be quiet and listen," Deimos said.

A tall, thin black man in his late forties was speaking with a teenage girl with pink skin and pinker hair. She wore rings along the lobes of each ear and through one nostril and had tattoos up and down her arms.

"I don't know, Benny," the teen said as Benny opened one of the kennels and brought out a Pitbull. "I don't see the point."

"Listen, Tiffany. I was like you when I was young." Benny put the dog on a leash and gave it to Tiffany to hold. "I floated around with no sense of purpose, with no real understanding of anything." He took a broom and started cleaning out the kennel while the girl watched. "I tried to kill myself once. My family was never there for me. I got into drugs. I stole money to pay for the drugs and ended up in jail." He swept litter onto a dustpan and emptied it into a plastic bin. "Then I came here. I learned how to take care of these dogs, how to train them, how to read them, and how to partner them with the right human companions. The joy I bring to both the people and the dogs on adoption day—it's like no drug I've ever known. It fills me with a sense of purpose. That's what you need, too. If not here, well, somewhere else. What do you love?"

"Nothing. I don't care about anything. I don't have any friends. I didn't finish school. There's no hope for me, Benny. You're just wasting your breath."

Deimos panicked when Hope left their huddle in the sky to fly closer to the teen.

Hope! Come back! What are you doing? Deimos said to her telepathically, as he followed on her heels.

I'm helping.

Deimos and Phobos exchanged looks of bewilderment.

"How's she *helping*?" Phobos asked.

"I wish you had faith in yourself, Tiffany," Benny said. "Hand me that hose."

Tiffany reached over and picked up a garden hose and handed it to Benny.

"Turn it on, will you? On low."

The girl walked the dog over to a water faucet, where the hose was connected, and turned on the water.

"Good. Turn it off," Benny called out after a few minutes.

Then the girl helped Benny to put the dog into the clean kennel.

"Everybody loves something," Benny said. "Maybe you haven't lived long enough to find it."

"I love jewelry," she said. "I took a class once, a long time ago, to learn how to make it. The teacher said I was good."

"There you go. Make jewelry," Benny said.

"Yeah, right. I wouldn't know where to start."

"Then let's find out together," Benny said. "But first, we need to finish cleaning these kennels."

Hope waved a hand at her sister, beckoning her to join. The two little winged cherubs hovered over Tiffany while she helped Benny with the other kennels. Deimos saw a change in the teen's attitude. Whether it was Benny's encouragement or the effects of Faith and Hope, or a combination, Deimos didn't know.

"I think we're going to have to get them each a dog," Phobos said, hovering in the air beside him.

"Where are we going to keep them? Not in the London flat, and certainly not on Mount Olympus."

"When I was down in the belly of Gaia, one of the Fates, Clotho, spoke to me, telepathically," Phobos said.

"Really? Why? What did she say?"

"She told me to keep Faith close to me. That we'd be out soon."

"That was rich, considering that they were the ones who put you there."

"She also said that she had a surprise for us. She told me what it was. And believe me, there's room for a couple of dogs."

Ellie rode in the limo toward her mother's house, where her husbands and daughters would meet her. Her hands were sweaty, and her heart was beating fast. When the girls arrived, each holding a dog in her arms, Ellie turned to Phobos and Deimos for an explanation.

"I'd like to see *you* tell them no to anything," Phobos said.

"We told them we would consider it," Deimos said. "We haven't decided anything."

Ellie shook her head. "Like there's any way we're going to be able to take them back *now*."

"Can we just get on with it?" Phobos asked. "Should I knock, or will you?"

"I can't wait to meet Grandma in person," Hope said. "She sounds nice in her prayers."

"She prays to you?" Ellie asked as they walked up the cracked sidewalk.

"Every day," Hope said.

"Me, too," Faith said.

"Did you find a house for them?" Deimos asked.

Ellie took a deep breath and knocked. "As a matter of fact, I did."

C H A P T E R   E I G H T E E N

Castle in the Clouds

I can't believe you talked my mom into letting Dominique and Jonivan adopt dogs," Ellie said to her husbands and daughters as they flew home toward Mount Olympus after a full day in New Orleans.

"They certainly have the room for them now," Deimos pointed out.

"I hope they like the mansion," Ellie said. "They seemed to, after the shock wore off. Don't you think?"

"Once we moved some personal items from her old house into the new rooms, it felt more like home," Deimos said.

"Give them time," Phobos said. "It's a lot to get used to."

"I wonder which doggies they're going to choose," Faith said. "There were so many cute ones."

"I hope they pick Sparky," Hope said. "I almost chose him and now feel bad that we couldn't take three."

"We don't even have a place for *two*," Ellie said as they approached the gates. "I don't think your daddies thought this through."

"Give us a little more credit," Phobos said.

Ellie studied Phobos's face. "What are you up to?"

Phobos shrugged.

She turned to Deimos.

"Don't look at me," he said. "I don't know anything. Apparently, the Fates have a surprise for us."

"And it's not through these gates," Phobos said. "Follow me."

Phobos led them higher into the clouds, not far from where Cupid and Psyche lived, to a mountain with a castle that Ellie had never seen before.

"What's this?" she asked as they landed on the mountainside.

The castle sat high on the mountain peak. Unlike Cupid and Psyche's, which was stout and golden, this castle was tall and narrow and made of white stone that sparkled like diamonds. Three stair towers were topped with gray spires, and each spire held a golden orb on its point. The body of the castle was at least three stories high and had a gray roof with four gables with arched windows and gray shutters.

A golden-paved sidewalk curved along the mountainside, meandering through a lovely front garden of white and yellow roses, before it reached a tall wooden door, painted gray to match the shutters on the gables. Flanking the door were two golden pillars topped with golden orbs, like those on top of the spires.

"Welcome home," Phobos said.

"What?" Ellie covered her mouth and glanced at the girls.

Faith and Hope gazed up at the castle with wide eyes.

"It's beautiful," Faith said.

"I can't believe we get to live here," Hope said. "Buster, look at your house. Isn't it amazing?"

"Can we go inside?" Faith asked, holding her dog, Fluffy, on her hip.

"Let's go," Deimos said.

Ellie followed the girls inside. The entrance had high ceilings with balconies from the second and third floor overlooking it and the gorgeous stone floor. One stair tower was off to the left and a second was off to the right. Straight ahead was a grand room with large windows on either side of a stone fireplace. The windows provided amazing views of the clouds below.

Behind the tower to the left was an enormous kitchen and connecting dining room with coffered ceilings. Behind the tower to the right was the master bedroom and bath.

The girls flew up the stairs with their dogs in tow to choose their bedrooms while Ellie, Phobos, and Deimos studied every detail of their gorgeous rooms on the first floor.

"I can't believe this is ours," Ellie said again and again.

Strangely, there was a knock at the front door.

"Who could that be?" Deimos said.

"Maybe Cupid and Psyche," Phobos said as he flew to the door.

Phobos opened the enormous door, which was at least eight feet tall and five feet wide, to reveal a crowd of gods standing outside.

Deimos flew to his brother's side and looked out at the gathering of gods. "What's this?"

Faith and Hope had flown down the stairs with their dogs to see what was happening.

"Your housewarming party," Aphrodite said, looking contrite. "Do you mind if we come inside?"

"We bring gifts," Ares added, perhaps to increase the chances of gaining entry.

Deimos turned to Ellie. "Should we let them in?"

"Yes," she said. "They're family, remember? And family members always deserve a second chance."

They gathered in the grand great room, which had enough seats for everyone.

Once they were settled, Zeus stood up, and helped his wife, Hera, to her feet. "We want to make amends. We know we've wronged you. No matter how much we justified it to ourselves, and we know there's nothing we can do to truly make amends for all we put you through, but we hope you'll see our gift as a start."

Zeus pointed to the back windows, where a swimming pool, the shape of a serpent, appeared, connected to what appeared to be a hot tub. The deck around the pool was made of stone encrusted with flakes of gold. Lawn furniture, made of gold and fine cushions, surrounded the pool. A peacock fountain was erected where the tail of the serpent curled on one end.

"It's beautiful!" Ellie cried.

Zeus and Hera took a seat as Poseidon and Amphitrite rose from theirs.

Poseidon glared at Zeus and said, "I suppose my brother has given you a fine body of water, but we have something better. Circling this mountainside, you will now find rivers and the clearest springs, full of life, surrounding your home. You'll find waterfalls that put the Niagara Falls to shame. You can fish, swim, explore, relax, and bathe to your heart's content."

"Buster, did you hear that?" Hope cried with excitement.

Faith clapped her hands. "I can't wait!"

Poseidon gave Zeus a haughty smile before he and Amphitrite returned to their seats.

Athena and Hephaestus were next.

"I built you a golden chariot," Hephaestus said.

"What?" Ellie was super pumped to have a car of her own. "Thank you!"

"And I found you the best horses for pulling it," Athena said.

"Psyche and I erected a barn and garage for them," Cupid added.

"Horses?" the girls cried.

"Two mares," Athena said. "Their names are Fame and Fortune."

Deimos laughed. "That's perfect for little goddesses named Faith and Hope."

Hecate and Demeter stood as Athena and Hephaestus took their seats.

"I planted you an herb garden," Hecate said.

"And I created a magical orchard," Demeter said. "You'll find the best apples, pears, oranges, lemons, peaches, and pecans on earth on your very own mountaintop."

"Oh, my gods!" Phobos said rubbing his belly. "I love oranges. Thank you."

"And thanks for the herbs," Deimos said to Hecate. "I love to cook with them."

"You cook?" Ellie asked.

"Yes, I do," Deimos said.

"Let's say that he *experiments*," Phobos clarified.

"That brings me to my gift," Hestia said. "I've filled your kitchen with all the best cookware, along with a book of my favorite recipes. I've even stocked your pantry with basic staples, so you can start right away. I've enchanted the pantry, so you'll never run out. That's how I do it on Mount Olympus."

"I'm suddenly quite hungry," Phobos said.

"Thank you, Hestia," Ellie said. "I can't wait to learn and to teach the girls."

"We'll be sure and invite you over for dinner," Deimos added.

Hades and Persephone flew to the center of the room. "You can never be too careful with visitors. Persephone and I, along with our Underworld family, have erected a golden fence that surrounds your entire estate. It has a front and back gate that can only be entered when one of you grant the visitor permission. The rest of the fence is impenetrable—as strong as a fortress."

Deimos wondered if Hades was the exception. Perhaps he had rigged it so that he could spy on their family from beneath the helm. Rather than mention his suspicions, he said, "Thank you, Lord Hades and Lady Persephone. Thank Hip and Than and the Furies for us, too."

"Speaking of visitors," Persephone said. "I hear one at the front gate now. I think it's the minotaur."

Deimos flew to the front door, and sure enough, about a hundred yards across the mountaintop, Asterion and Ariadne stood outside his new golden gate.

"Come in!" Deimos shouted.

A moment later, the minotaur and his sister entered bearing gifts.

"A golden compass," Asterion said. "To help you find your way."

"I brought lavender," Ariadne said. "Put it in your bath or in a diffuser to help you rest."

"How thoughtful!" Ellie said, taking the gifts from their newest guests and putting them on a side table.

"I have something for you, too," Apollo said, handing Ellie a globe. It looked like a Christmas globe, but with glitter and liquid inside.

"It's beautiful," Ellie said.

"What is it?" Faith asked.

"Shake it," Apollo said.

Ellie gave it a shake, and when the glittery dust settled, she saw her mother, sister, and nephew walking the grounds of the dog shelter.

"Whenever you need to see your mortal family," Apollo said, "just give that a shake."

Deimos clapped Apollo on the back. "I didn't know you had it in you, uncle."

"Oh, look!" Hope cried. "Grandma is talking to Benny Munos! He recognizes her!"

"What are you talking about?" Ellie asked.

"Benny is Dominique's biological father," Deimos said. "Hecate found him. He's a good man, Works at the shelter."

Faith clapped her hands. "Grandma's introducing him to Auntie Dominique!"

"Aww," Ellie said. "Benny's crying tears of joy."

"So are Auntie and Grandma," Hope said. "How exciting! Now, if only they'll choose Sparky!"

Phobos laughed. "You don't want much, do you, kid?"

"I guess I already have everything a girl could ever want!"

"Not an immortal girl," Artemis said. "My gift to you is immortality for your dogs. That way, they can live with you forever."

Faith and Hope flew into the air and turned somersaults. Then they flew back to Artemis and gave her hugs.

"Looks like you're the favorite aunt," Phobos said.

"And I'm about to be the favorite uncle," Hermes said.

"Don't be too sure about that," Apollo said with a laugh.

"As a god of many talents, my gift to you is two-fold," Hermes said. "To help you with your speed, I've put up a softball field further down the mountain, on a flat clearing, just inside the back fence."

A softball field?" Ellie exclaimed gleefully. "Here?"

"I can help you teach the girls to play," Hermes said. "I bet we can recruit Asterion to join."

"You bet," the minotaur said.

"Oh, wow!" Faith cried. "That sounds like a fun time."

"It does!" Hope agreed. "I bet Fluffy and Buster would like that, too, wouldn't you, boys?"

The pups each gave a single bark.

Deimos didn't say it aloud, but he hoped to one day bring the Garcias up to the mountain to see how the gods play softball. He'd have to erase their memories, of course, but it would still be fun.

"Hahaha!" Hermes mussed the girls' hair. "And my other gift to you is this. He pulled pipes from thin air and presented one to each of the girls. I made them myself. I'll teach you how to play. You can experiment on your own until then."

The girls flew around the room as they blew into their pipes, making a horrendous racket.

"Thanks a lot, Hermes," Phobos said sardonically. "Don't forget that Karma's a bitch."

Hermes threw back his head and guffawed.

Aphrodite and Ares now flew to the center of the room.

"We've given this a lot of thought," Ares said.

"We feel bad for all that happened," Aphrodite said with tears in her eyes. "I hope you believe we thought we were doing what was best."

Deimos sucked in his lips and nodded. His brothers were silent. Ellie seemed to have a hard time meeting Aphrodite's gaze.

"Anyway, you boys know how often your mother and I like to visit Paris," Ares said. "We've bought you a flat up there, too, big enough for all five of you."

"Thanks," Deimos said. "That will come in handy, since the London flat is relatively small."

"Small?" Ellie said with a wry grin. "It's still bigger than the house I grew up in."

"We hope you enjoy it," Aphrodite said. "And we hope that, one day, you'll let us back into your hearts.

Deimos nodded. "Thanks again."

That won't happen anytime soon, Phobos prayed to Deimos.

Let's not put a damper on the day, Deimos prayed back.

You're right, for once.

You say that a lot, you know.

Ellie cleared her throat. "I know we didn't get off to a great start, but I thank each and every one of you for your generous gifts. My daughters and I are excited about joining the pantheon. In fact, it's probably about time we got to work."

The gods applauded Ellie's speech and said their goodbyes.

At the door, Ellie stopped Persephone and asked, "Is it true, what the Fates said? Did you allow yourself to be swallowed by Gaia?"

"Yes," Persephone said.

"Why?" Deimos asked.

Persephone glanced at her husband and then said, "Lachesis told me that getting swallowed for all eternity would save my husband, so I did it."

Hades kissed her cheek. Then he said, "You may not be looking for marital advice, but here's something to think about: a selfish husband is a lonely one."

Then he and Persephone followed the other gods from the mountain.

Deimos was glad when the five of them had the house to themselves.

A little while later, the girls took the dogs to meet Fame and Fortune, so Deimos turned to Ellie and Phobos. "Before you go to perform your duties among the mortals, I think we need to work something out."

"What do you mean?" Ellie asked.

"We need to get our groove down, while the girls are occupied."

Phobos grinned. "Bro', I was thinking the very same thing."

Ellie joined her husbands in their new master bedroom. She sent a telepathic prayer to the girls that she and their daddies were going to be busy for a while and shouldn't be disturbed.

The fourposter bed sat on a wooden frame and was thick with mattresses and sheets made of the finest silk.

"We haven't had time to practice," Deimos said. "And the last time, well, it ended way too quickly. I want us to take our time."

Phobos grinned. "I'm down for practicing. Ellie?"

"I'm down," she said, already aroused by the idea of it.

"Let's set the mood." Deimos made a fire in the hearth.

Phobos produced some music. It was classic rock—Deimos's favorite.

"Juicy Jenkins is great music for dancing," Phobos said, "but this is better for what we're about to do to you."

Ellie licked her lips and trembled with excitement.

She was startled when her blouse and bra vanished.

Deimos approached her and gently touched her nipples. They responded to his fingers. He smiled down at her. She felt a little weak at the knees as he licked her lips and then gently kissed her breast.

From behind, Phobos removed her trousers and panties before he glided a hand from the middle of her thigh and up toward her crotch, where she was already wet with anticipation. As one hand caressed her between the legs, another caressed the curves of her bottom.

Then Deimos held her breasts while he kissed her again, harder, more fiercely and passionately. His lips moved down her neck and to her breast again. She sighed with pleasure as her hands explored his muscular chest, back, shoulders, bottom, and then worked down his abs to find him hard. She glided her hand up and down, causing him to gasp, while Phobos used his hands to bring her to the brink of ecstasy.

Not wanting to climax yet, she turned around to kiss Phobos, stopping his hands from performing their magic. She explored his back and chest while Deimos held her bottom and kissed the back of her neck. When she found Phobos, hard and wet, he groaned. He looked at her with smoldering eyes before he pressed his mouth hard against hers.

"I was going to let you enter her this time," Deimos whispered. "But…"

"Go for it, bro'," Phobos said. "I'm good. I'm so good right now."

Deimos entered Ellie from behind. Pleasure pulsed through her. She moved her body in rhythm with Deimos as he rammed himself against her. She also glided her hands up and down on Phobos, who pinched her nipples so hard, she thought they'd bleed. But it hurt in the most delightful way.

"Take your time," Phobos said. "Don't rush it."

"I'm at a good place," Deimos said. "I can hold it."

"Oh, gods," Ellie said. "I'm about to explode."

"Make it last," Phobos said, pinching her harder. "I'm on the brink, but I want it to last."

They rubbed themselves against one another for as long as they could, before Ellie cried out, unable to stop herself from going over the edge. Deimos was right there with her. It was if her cries took him over the edge, too. As the pulse between her legs raged for a few intensely pleasurable moments, Phobos came, too.

"I think we've got the hang of this," Deimos said.

"For the first time, bro', I think you're right."

Ellie giggled as she made her way to her master bath and turned on the hot water. It was like a spa, reminding her of the bedroom suite she stayed in at Cupid's castle. She couldn't believe it was hers and that this was now her life.

When the large tub was filled, she climbed in. Her husbands joined her with goblets of wine, candles, and oranges.

"I wonder how the girls are doing," she said as she rested her head on the marble ledge of the tub.

"I just checked on them," Phobos said. "When I went to get the oranges. Cupid is teaching them how to groom Fame and Fortune."

"What a life," she said. "But after we rest, we really must get to work. There's one person, in particular, whose prayers have been desperate. He needs my help and could use the help of Hope and Faith, too."

CHAPTER NINETEEN

The Goddesses of Hope, Faith, and Lost Causes

Ellie had been listening to the prayers of this one young man, only a year younger than she, named Paul, who'd been praying to her night and day.

I'm on my last rope. Hell. What rope? There's nothing left to hold onto.

From his prayers, Ellie had learned that he had five younger siblings—two brothers and three sisters—who depended on him. Their ages ranged from fourteen to six. Paul was responsible for feeding them and getting them to school. When they came home with lice one day, he was the one who had to treat their hair. When the pantry was empty and his parents had nothing to feed them, Paul found a second job to help out.

His parents worked, but they had dug themselves into a financial hole they couldn't climb out of. For years, when they couldn't find work, they used credit cards to feed their family. But then their credit was shot. When Paul turned nineteen, they got a credit card in his name and ran it up. And when their only car had broken down six months ago, they took out a car loan in Paul's name, so they had a way to get to work. His parents couldn't keep up with the payments, so Paul's credit was trashed, along with his chances of getting a loan to go to college.

His prayers to Ellie broke her heart.

I want to be there for my family, but I want to break out of this damn cycle of poverty and go to college. If I stay and work and help my family, nothing's gonna ever change. If I leave, I might make something of myself and, in turn, be able to do more for them. But what will happen to my six-year-old sister in the meantime? My parents don't seem to care. If they do, they have a horrible way of showing it. Maybe they're too tired and broken. Maybe they've given up. What do I do?

Then, three days ago, Paul prayed that his family was about to be evicted from their apartment, because they were three months behind on their rent.

Paul said that he wondered if he and his brothers and sisters would be better off dead.

I'm losing hope, he prayed. *I used to have faith in myself, but now I don't think I can do shit for my family or for myself. I'm just another piece of crap in the world with no chance to survive.*

Ellie found Hope and Faith playing in the yard with Buster and Fluffy.

"We heard," Hope said. "Are you finally ready to go?"

Ellie was taken aback. "What do you mean, am I *finally* ready?"

"We should have gone to Paul a long time ago," Faith said. "And there are others who need us. Can we go now?"

Ellie nodded. "Your daddies are off doing their work, so it's time we went and did ours."

With Hope on one side of her and Faith on the other, the goddess of lost causes flew from their mountain castle toward America, to Detroit, Michigan.

Hope and Faith hovered above the dilapidated apartment complex, trying to inspire Paul and his family, while Ellie looked around the neighborhood and surrounding area for a way to help. What could she do to get Paul and his family out of their deep hole?

She couldn't just hand out money to every mortal in need, because, as Deimos had once told her, that would only cause inflation in the long run. She had to find a way to help the mortals to help themselves.

Ellie searched the area for days, listening in on conversations, hoping to find a solution. On the fourth day, she heard a prayer from an old man, and inspiration struck.

The old man lived in a wealthier district of Detroit, but he had no relatives to help him. He didn't want to leave his home of fifty years, where he raised his boys—whom he'd unfortunately, outlived. He needed someone to buy his groceries, take him to doctor appointments, and offer companionship.

Ellie had to find a way to bring Paul and Thomas together. Thomas needed to see what a good and trusting soul Paul was. Ellie hoped that, eventually, Thomas would want to help Paul and his family by becoming their benefactor.

One day, about a week later, Ellie managed to trick Paul into getting off the train at the wrong stop and to walk, aimlessly lost in thought for hours, toward Thomas's neighborhood. Hope and Faith helped her to get the old man out on his front lawn, to get his mail and his newspaper, at the same time Paul was walking up his street, trying to figure out where the heck he was.

Ellie made Thomas's mailbox lid get stuck. Paul noticed him struggling.

"Can I help you with that, sir?" Paul asked.

"Why, thank you," Thomas said.

Paul yanked the mailbox lid open and handed Thomas the mail.

"I've never seen you around here before," Thomas said. "Are you new to the neighborhood?"

"No, sir. I'm lost."

"You want me to call you a cab?"

"Unfortunately, I ain't got no money, sir. I just got off the train at the wrong stop and somehow ended up here. Can you point me in the direction of the train?"

"You're a long way off from the train. Are you not feeling well?"

"I have a headache but I'm okay."

"Do you want to sit down and have a glass of water?"

"No, sir. I don't want to be a bother."

"I'll make a deal with you," Thomas said. "I can't drive anymore, and I need some groceries. If you'll drive me in my car to the store and drive me back, I'll give you money for a cab and then some—for your time and trouble. Like I said, the train is quite a walk from here."

"You got yourself a deal," Paul said.

Hope and Faith swarmed around both men before they flew away with Ellie, feeling satisfied that they'd put their plan in motion.

It took several months, but Paul and Thomas eventually worked their way into one another's hearts, and Thomas invited Paul's family over to celebrate Thanksgiving, so Thomas wouldn't be alone. Paul made sure that his parents didn't take advantage of the old man, and Thomas made sure that Paul's siblings didn't starve. The following year, after Paul had been working for Thomas for eight months, Thomas offered to pay for Paul to go to the community college.

It wasn't Harvard, but it was a start.

Over the years, Faith and Hope followed their mother around, helping people out of their despair. And then they'd come home to their castle in the clouds and make memories together with Phobos and Deimos, Buster and Fluffy, and Fame and Fortune. They were visited often by Cupid and Psyche, who soon had a child of their own.

Phobos and Deimos eventually forgave their parents. They had to, because they worked almost every day with Ares, and they couldn't carry a grudge forever. But Ellie had a feeling that her husbands looked to her and to Hope and Faith for a real sense of family. And Ellie made it her mission to make them feel loved and appreciated every day of their lives.

One evening, the five of them were at home, and Deimos had just cooked something for dinner using a recipe from Hestia.

The girls had continued to grow but had come to what seemed like a standstill at puberty. The five of them sat around the table to eat.

"The last time Deimos tried to cook," Phobos said, "the fire trucks ruined it."

The girls giggled.

"I burned a lot of calories that day," Deimos said.

Phobos clapped his brother on the back. "Too bad we never got to eat them!"

"This chicken is tasty," Ellie said. "Deimos has improved."

Deimos shot her a smile before taking a sip of his wine.

"I have a question," Faith said. "I overhear mortals debating it all the time. What comes first—the chicken or the egg?"

Phobos mussed Faith's hair and said, "I don't know. Order it from Amazon and let's see."

THE END

Thank you for reading my story. If you enjoyed it, please consider leaving a review. Reviews help other readers to find my books, which helps me.

Please enjoy the first chapter of a book that shares the same world, *Charon's Quest*.

Chapter One

Off the boat," Hades demanded.

Charon looked up at his master, unsure if he'd heard him correctly.

"I've had a visit from Apollo." Hades crossed his arms and widened his stance. "Your future is unclear, but your demise is certain if you do not leave my kingdom."

"Leave, my lord?" Charon's bones were tired, and it pained him to speak.

"Haven't you noticed how aged and withered you've become? You're no good to me like this."

"I don't understand."

"My dear Charon, why are you the only one among us who has aged like an old man?"

Charon glanced at his trembling, bony hands and wrinkled, spotted flesh.

"Apollo saw the answer in a vision," Hades said. "Off the boat. Follow me."

Charon rarely left the skiff—only to sleep in his abode on the night of each full moon. When he did leave the boat, he flew, because to walk was painful.

He followed Hades down the winding corridor of the Underworld along the river of fire. He did not need the soft glow from the Phlegethon to see his master walking ahead of him, upright, muscled, virile. Unlike Hades, Charon's frail back was bowed—even in flight—and every bone trembled with old age.

So, he was to get his youth back, eh? Charon couldn't care less about it. And the last thing he wanted was to visit the Upperworld, where he hadn't set foot since the beginning of time. Why did Apollo have to stir up trouble for him?

Hades rounded the corner and entered the foyer of his and his queen's main palace. "Have a seat."

Charon flew to one of the oversized wooden chairs gathered around a golden table. He couldn't recall ever sitting in this room before.

Hades paced across from him. "I'll allow you to retain your powers, as long as you don't abuse them. You'll need money…and better clothes. Perhaps a cane."

Charon's old robes were immediately replaced by dark gray trousers and a pale button-down shirt with long sleeves. His old rubber boots disappeared, and in in their place were short black boots made of leather. A black wooden cane appeared in his hand and a gray fedora on his head.

"That's better," Hades said.

This was all too much. Charon already missed his robes.

"I didn't think it possible for a god to die, my lord."

"You seem to be the exception, my friend." Hades continued to pace, and now he scratched his beard. "Apollo says it's because you vicariously experience the lives of each soul that boards your skiff."

Charon rubbed his temple, where a new pain was forming. While it was true that the lives of each soul flashed before his eyes, it hadn't occurred to him that his aging was the result.

"Might Apollo be mistaken?" Charon asked.

"I suppose there's a first time for everything," Hades replied. "Even so, we should err on the side of caution."

Charon bit his trembling lip.

Hades stopped pacing to study him. "I would think you'd be grateful for the chance to go out on adventures of your own, for a change. Why so glum?"

"Glum seems hardly the right adjective, my lord. Terrified is more like it."

Hades sat in the chair opposite him and furrowed his brow. "You forget who you are. Why should a god be terrified to go among mortals?"

"I'm a creature of habit. I like my life just as it is. I've never been anywhere but here, in your kingdom. This is my home. I prefer it to anyplace else."

Hades laughed and clapped him hard on the shoulder, nearly cracking his clavicle in half. "My dear Charon, it's not like you won't be coming back. Think of this as an opportunity to spread your wings."

"I haven't got wings, my lord."

"Metaphorically speaking."

Charon sighed, realizing there was no getting out of it. "What would you have me do?"

"That's more like it. Chin up! I'm truly happy for you to have this chance. You can travel the world, meet interesting people, and do exciting things."

Charon would rather have none of it.

Hades climbed to his feet and resumed his pacing and the scratching of his beard. "Where should I send you first? One of the great cities, perhaps?"

"I know little of the Upperworld, my lord. I've come to understand bits of it from the souls I ferry."

"And from those bits, aren't you curious about the world? Isn't there something you wonder about?"

There was one thing he wondered about. He never imagined he'd have the chance to experience it.

"The cinema," Charon said. "I wonder about the cinema."

The corners of Hades's mouth curled up into a gleeful smile. "Well, then. I know exactly where to send you, my old friend."

* * *

Charon emerged at night amidst a bustling city. Although he'd retained his godly powers, he didn't need night vision to see the automobiles crawling by on the streets, or the people walking briskly to who knew where. Nor did he need the starlight, invisible here beneath the smog. The ample light emanating from the signs, streetlamps, and headlights was more than enough to make everything about this crowded, dirty place visible.

He hobbled along with his cane and entered the cinema. While he'd retained his powers, Hades had warned him against using them. His lord had said that if mortals discovered they had a god among them, Charon would have no chance to enjoy his experience. The constant requests and complaints would sabotage his efforts at happiness.

The last thing Charon wanted was to be bothered by people.

He reached into his trouser pocket for one of the golden coins given to him by Hades and handed it to the clerk.

"Um, cash or credit card, sir," the boy said as he turned over the coin.

"The gold is more than enough for a ticket," Charon said, compelling the pimpled youth to cooperate, since there were no other mortals around to witness it.

"Which show, sir?"

"You choose."

"What genre do you like?" the boy asked. "Drama? Comedy? Suspense?"

Charon grinned. "I like it all."

The clerk handed over a ticket and Charon walked past.

The theater was half-empty when Charon entered and found a seat on the end of the first row, away from others. As the movie played, he forgot where and when he was as he ran the full gamut of emotions. He laughed, he cried, and he gasped in surprise, and he cried again at the end.

When the film ended, he used his cane and the arm of his seat to pull himself to his feet. Getting up was much more difficult than getting down. Among the others leaving the room, he plodded along, deciding to go to the room next door, where another film was about to begin. No one stopped him. He sat in the same row, same seat.

The comedy left him in a delightful mood. He decided to try one more film. The movie in the room next door had already begun. He found his seat and watched.

The third film left him feeling terrified. His hands were shaking—worse than usual—and he could barely breathe. Wasn't the purpose of coming to the Upperworld to restore his youth and vitality? And yet, he felt worse than ever.

As the others in the theater made their way to the exit and the lights turned on, Charon sat there, holding his chest. There was a new pain there—a tightness that left him crippled.

"Sir? Are you okay?" a woman asked him.

Before Charon could reply, Thanatos appeared beside the woman. Now that Charon was focused on regaining his youth, he was struck by the disparity between his shriveled, wrinkled flesh and the youthful vibrancy of Thanatos. His bright blue eyes shone down at him beneath wavy, dark hair. His complexion was flawless, his shoulders and chest broad and strong.

"Have you come for me?" Charon asked the youthful god.

"Excuse me?" the woman asked.

The woman couldn't see Death.

Thanatos frowned. "We need to talk. Come with me."

Taking him by the arm, Thanatos god-traveled with Charon from the cinema to a brightly lit hotel room with two beds, a sofa, and a table and chairs.

"I just collected a soul from this room," Thanatos said. "The body is in the bathtub."

"Won't there be a stench?"

"You can book your own room downstairs," Thanatos said. "But first, we need to talk. Have a seat."

Charon eased himself into one of the two wooden chairs beside the table.

"When you said you liked the cinema, Hades thought you might enjoy a tour of Universal Studios," Thanatos said. "That's why he sent you here, to L.A."

"A tour?"

"To learn how the movies are made."

Charon waved his hand at the wrist. "I don't care about that. I only care about watching them."

"That's no different than seeing the lives of others flash before your eyes," Thanatos pointed out. "It won't help."

"Hmm."

Charon looked up at his old friend, comforted by his presence. They'd spent most of their time on the skiff together. Thanatos—or Than, as most of the Underworld gods called him—brought the souls and remained aboard until the dead reached their final resting place— whether that was the Fields of Elysium for the good, Tartarus for the wicked, or Erebus for those needing time to heal. Charon had rarely exchanged words with him in the last century or two, because it pained him to speak; but it hadn't always been so.

"You need to experience life," Than said. "I envy you this chance. You need to take full advantage."

Charon chuckled.

"What's so funny?"

"The irony," Charon said. "Death telling me about life."

"If not a tour, then what?" Than asked.

"Take me somewhere," Charon said. "Be my guide."

"You know mortals can't tolerate me," Than replied.

"I'd forgotten. They drop dead in your presence."

"Not immediately, but still."

"I don't like people anyway," Charon said. "Take me someplace where I can have adventures away from others."

Thanatos grimaced. "That's rather missing the point, isn't it?"

"I disagree." Charon climbed to his feet, which wasn't easy. "Put me on a boat on a river somewhere. You have the remarkable ability to be everywhere at once. Come with me."

Than crossed his arms. "I'll make a deal with you."

"Now you sound like your father."

"I'll keep an eye on you, until you find a companion," Than said. "You'll need American money—not the gold my father gave you."

Than handed him a wallet made of leather. Charon opened it to find it stuffed with pieces of green paper.

"That's a magical wallet," Than said. "It won't run out of money and will supply you with the right currency for whatever country you happen to visit."

"What do I need it for?"

"Use it to buy things—like food and clothes. Don't wear the same trousers and shirt each day."

Charon rolled his eyes. "You want me to go shopping?"

"And meet someone," Than said.

"That'll be easy," Charon said sarcastically.

"Then I'll put you and him—or her—on a boat on a river of your choosing."

"How do you expect me to do that? It'll take time to get someone to trust me enough to go on a trip like that. Your deal is worthless."

Thanatos put a hand on Charon's shoulder. "This city is full of people. Surely you can make friends with one of them."

"I don't know where to start."

Thanatos turned away. "Try the bar downstairs."

* * *

Charon took the elevator to the first floor and found the bar across from the lobby. A group in their mid to late thirties sat together at one table, but, otherwise, the place was quiet with a couple in a corner booth and two individuals sitting at either end of the bar.

Charon hobbled across the room to sit on a stool at the center of the bar.

"What can I get for you, sir?" The bartender was a young woman in her twenties with long, black curls pinned behind her ears and a chocolate complexion with rosy cheeks.

Charon had only ever drunk ambrosia and the wine of Dionysus. "You choose."

The young woman smiled. "Are you thirsty for something sweet or sour? Something stiff or weak?"

"Something stiff and not sweet."

"You'll want a shot of whiskey then," she said. "Do you have a favorite brand?"

Charon shook his head. "Give me your finest."

The spunky bartender poured him a glass and set it before him.

She watched as he put the glass to his lips and tasted the whiskey.

"Mmm." Charon gave her a smile. "This will do."

"You look familiar," the bartender said. "I think I've seen you before."

Charon squinted at the inscription on her nametag. "That's unlikely, Matilda."

The bartender poured another drink and delivered it to the man at the far end of the bar. When she returned, she asked, "Are you from around here?"

"Nowhere near," he said before taking another sip of the smooth whiskey.

"I know I've seen you before," she said. "I bet I'll figure it out before the night's over."

Charon lifted his glass, as if to toast her. "You do that."

Matilda left to attend to the large group. When she returned, she said to Charon, "Enjoy the quiet while you can. It's about to get busy in here."

"What makes you say that?" he asked.

"The parade is nearly over."

Charon frowned. "Parade?"

"Dia de los Muertos. You must have passed it on your way here. It's been going on for three days."

"The Day of the Dead?" Charon had never heard of such a thing.

"I guess you *aren't* from around here." Matilda poured five drinks and then delivered them to the large group.

Charon now had a vague memory of having learned about the celebration from some of the souls who boarded his skiff. Halloween. Melinoe's night. Some of the dead who'd managed to escape Thanatos were rounded up and brought home. But the mortals believed the dead were released from their resting place and allowed to walk among them. Centuries ago, people disguised themselves out of fear, to blend in with the other ghosts. Somehow this tradition had become an elaborate, week-long festival, complete with music, art, dancing, costumes, and—according to Matilda—parades.

He wondered if it had been Apollo or Hades who'd decided to send Charon to the Upperworld during Dia de los Muertos. And, whoever it was, did he think he was being funny?

When Matilda returned behind the bar, she took a rectangular, flat device from her trouser pocket and held it to her ear. Although she spoke into it softly, Charon could hear her every word. He realized she was speaking to someone on a phone.

Matilda was being told that someone named Kayla didn't have much time to live, that Matilda needed to prepare herself and visit the hospital as soon as she was able.

The bartender wiped tears from her cheeks and returned the phone to her trouser pocket. When she noticed Charon's empty glass, she asked, "Ready for another?"

Charon gave her a nod and watched her fill his glass before bringing it to his lips. Matilda's dramatic change in mood unsettled him, so he said, "Death isn't so bad, you know."

She stopped mixing her next concoction and narrowed her eyes at him. "You sure have good ears for a person your age."

He shrugged. "What can I say? That's true."

He took another sip of the whiskey, enjoying the numbing effect it was having on his aches and pains.

The bartender continued mixing her drinks but said, "I'm not worried for Kayla. I know she's going to a good place. I'm worried for her parents and brother." Tears fell down the young woman's lovely face. "And I'm worried for me, because she was my friend."

Charon didn't know what to say. How could the loss of one person affect so many people?

"It may not seem like it now," he began. "But life will go on for the rest of you. I doubt you'll have any trouble making a new friend."

Matilda's face twisted into a deeper frown as more tears leaked from the corners of her eyes. Clearly, he'd said the wrong thing.

Just then the glass doors to the street swung open, and a crowd of people with painted faces and jeweled costumes burst into the bar, filling the remaining tables and booths. Their faces were painted white and resembled skulls. Some of the women wore black veils with short dresses, while others wore paper flowers in their hair and long, colorful skirts. One of the men wore a sombrero and a black suit, while others were dressed in ragged clothing decorated with fake blood.

Matilda sighed, wiped her cheeks, and went to take their orders.

Charon watched the mortals dressed in their depictions of death and couldn't help but laugh at them. They must be desperate for an excuse to have a party. Then he supposed one had to pass the time somehow, so why should he judge them?

When Matilda returned with an air of exhaustion, Charon leaned over the bar and said, "This might not mean much to you, but I thought you should know that you are the first real person with whom I've ever had a conversation." He laid down a handful of cash from the wallet Thanatos had given him. "Thank you."

Matilda stared at the money as her mouth dropped open in surprise. "That's over two hundred dollars, sir."

"You keep the change," Charon said.

She covered his hand with hers as more tears slipped down her cheeks. "Your kindness couldn't have come at a better time. Thanks so much."

Then he heard her unwitting prayer to him: *You are the kindest person I've ever met.*

Charon, like the other gods, couldn't read the thoughts of mortals; however, when a person directed a prayer to him personally, wittingly or not, he could hear it clearly. Not wanting to give away his godly status, he ignored it.

As he stood from the stool to leave, he found it easier to move. Apparently, speaking with someone had worked wonders on him. He wondered what good it would do to speak to a group. Maybe interacting with more people would multiply the effect.

He crossed over to the painted faces gathered around the tables and waved.

"I hope you enjoy your celebration," he called out.

"Join us, Senor!" the man in the sombrero said to him. "Pull up a chair and have a drink on me!"

Charon would rather return to the lobby, rent a room, and retire in solitude, but because he hoped to regain more of his strength and stamina from the encounter, he accepted the young man's offer. A chair was brought over from another table and scooted into the middle of the group, where Charon sat, despite his misgivings.

"What are you drinking?" the man with the sombrero asked. "Bartender, please bring this man another of whatever he's having."

Matilda brought him another whiskey, and it went down smooth.

"Thank you," Charon said to the man with the sombrero.

"De nada, Senor," the man said. "So, tell me, do you have any advice to give for how to live a long and fruitful life?"

Charon scratched his head beneath his fedora as the others in the group grew quiet and waited for his answer. "Avoid Death."

His new companions broke out in boisterous laughter.

"Claro que si!" The man in the sombrero stood up and held his glass aloft. "A toast! May we all avoid death as long as humanly possible!"

"Cheers!" one of the women shouted.

"Cheers! To avoiding death!" another said.

The group clinked their glasses together and drank to the toast. Charon felt himself feeling more energetic. For the first time in centuries, he straightened his back in his chair.

After a few more minutes, he stood to leave, thanking the man in the sombrero for the drink. He waved goodbye to Matilda and had already reached the lobby when she rushed to his side and said, "You forgot your cane."

"Thank you," he said, as he took it from her—though he no longer needed it. Then he added, "I hope you'll get to see your friend once more before she dies."

"It's too late," Matilda said, fighting sobs. "I just received word. She's gone."

A feeling quite foreign to Charon compelled him to comfort the poor mortal. He put his arms around her and cupped the back of her head with his hand.

"Not gone," he said. "Just not here. She's somewhere else."

Matilda collapsed against him, and he was surprised that he could hold her weight. She was petite, but, before tonight, he could barely manage his own weight, much less that of another. More of his strength had returned.

He'd never held a living being against him like this. Her beating heart pounded against his, and her warm flesh was a comfort to him, even though he meant to comfort *her*. She smelled lovely. He felt as if he could hold her there, in the middle of the lobby, for a very long time.

"Thank you," she said when she pulled away. But when she met his gaze, her brows furrowed into an expression of perplexity.

"What's wrong?" he asked.

"Nothing." She continued to stare up at him. "It's just that, in this light, you seem much younger than I thought you were."

Charon turned to look at his reflection in the mirrored wall behind the front desk of the lobby. He was fully upright and less thin—more robust. He had more hair on his head beneath his hat, though it remained gray. Instead of a man on his death bed, he looked like a respectable man in his sixties. He rather liked the change.

"You're the reason for it," Charon said, turning to Matilda. "You make me feel like a younger man."

Matilda blushed and smiled. "Goodnight, sir." She turned to leave.

"Goodnight." He watched as she retreated to her place behind the bar.

Now a new feeling penetrated his heart. The only word he could think of to describe this new feeling was *longing*.

Chapter Two

Although it hadn't been a full moon—which was the usual time when he slept—Charon had returned to his room and had dozed off out of boredom. When sunlight trickled in through the curtains, he was brought from his dreams sooner than he'd wished. He'd been holding the bartender Matilda in his arms and comforting her.

He climbed from the bed, still wearing his shirt and trousers, to find his clothes wrinkled. He put on his hat and boots and headed out to the street to shop for new ones.

The delicious smells on the corner led him to a bakery, where he had a roll and coffee before continuing his journey. He felt better than he had in centuries. The cool morning air was crisp and invigorating, and the smog no longer bothered him.

As he passed a store window, he was surprised to see Matilda inside the shop. Instead of her black trousers, black blouse, and white apron from last night, she wore a pretty sweater, short skirt, and tall boots. Her long curly hair was pinned back on each side, showing off her nice cheek bones, as it had the night before. She was standing in front of a row of greeting cards and was picking through them.

He entered the shop and watched her as she opened one card, read it, laughed, and replaced it. Then she opened another and did the same. Her laughter, her bright face, and her sweet smile made him smile, too.

He felt frumpy and embarrassed by his wrinkled clothes, so he didn't try to speak with her. He turned and headed back out to the street.

He walked the streets for another hour, peering into shop windows but never venturing into them. Once, he stopped to speak to a shopkeeper on the sidewalk about the price of trousers; otherwise, he kept to himself. How was he supposed to find a companion to sail along a river with him in this crowded city? He had nothing to offer a friend and nothing to talk about. These people scurrying in and out of shops had nothing in common with him. In fact, he was all but invisible to them.

Maybe he'd have to forget the idea of boating on a river. Maybe he'd have to find adventures among the masses. But what? What was there to do other than shop and eat and tour theme parks? He had no interest in museums. He knew enough about human history and its art and culture from the memories of the souls in Hades. Was there anything worthwhile to occupy his time?

He was thinking of Matilda when he saw her again as she entered the double glass doors of an enormous corner building. It was a hospital.

Charon decided to follow her. Was she ill? Or was she going to pay her respects to her friend who'd passed the day before?

He followed her from a safe distance up a stairwell to the second floor. When she turned a corner, he nearly lost her, until he heard someone greet her. He continued down the hall toward the sound of her voice and flattened against the wall, out of sight, when he saw her standing at what must be a nurses' station, where a woman was handing Matilda a garment—what Charon believed was called "scrubs."

"Johnny's been asking for you," the woman said to Matilda. "He'll be glad to see you again."

"Why?" Matilda's face darkened. "Is it almost time?"

The woman behind the desk shrugged. "It's hard to tell. You know how it is. Could be hours, could be months."

Matilda slipped the green garment over her head and pushed her arms through its sleeves before saying, "I don't know how the families can take it."

"It's hard for the doctors, too," the other woman said. "You'll find out soon enough."

"Not that soon. I've got two more years before I can even begin my residency." Matilda continued down the hall. She looked cute with her short skirt jetting out from beneath the green top.

The other woman called out, "It goes by faster than you think."

Charon followed Matilda through a set of double doors, over which a sign read "Children's Ward."

When she entered a room, he waited outside the door to eavesdrop.

"Hey, Johnny," Matilda said.

Charon was expecting to hear a child's voice, but it was the low voice of a young man that answered. "There you are, Beautiful."

Matilda laughed.

Was this a boyfriend?

"I brought you a card," she said. "Open it."

Charon heard the slight tear of paper. Then there was nothing but the sound of the mortals breathing, until the young man burst into laughter.

"That's the best one yet," Johnny said. "Thanks."

"I love to see you laugh," Matilda said. "You're pretty darn handsome when you do."

There was an awkward silence, until Johnny said, "How's school?"

"It's killing me."

Johnny laughed.

"I'm sorry," Matilda said. "That was insensitive."

"Oh, stop," Johnny protested. "You don't have to walk on eggshells around me."

"School wouldn't be so bad if I didn't have to work late, standing on my feet all night," Matilda added. "I need more sleep."

"You can sleep when you're dead," Johnny said.

"Stop it."

"What? You started it."

"True." Then she said. "Well, your vitals look great. And your coloring looks better than it did last week. How do you feel?"

"Better now that you're here."

She laughed. "So much cheese! Ugh!"

"What? Are you vegan or something?"

Matilda laughed again. "You're cray-cray."

"What are you? Ancient? No one says that anymore."

"Oh, stop teasing me."

"But it's so much fun." Then, Johnny added, "Will you come back by after your rounds?"

"Of course, I will," Matilda said. "I told you. You're my favorite."

"I bet you say that to everyone," Johnny teased.

Charon heard the sound of a kiss. Was it on the cheek? The forehead? The lips?

"Maybe I do," Matilda teased. "See you later."

Charon realized Matilda was on her way out of the room, but not in time to react. She saw him, standing there in the hallway.

"Oh, hello," she said, recognizing him. "Wow."

He wasn't sure how to take her comment. "Wow?"

"The light in the hotel does *not* do you justice, sir," Matilda said. "Beneath these florescent lights, you look much younger."

"I was tired last night."

"And I see you're without your cane."

"A temporary injury," he quickly explained. "It seems I'm healed."

"Are you here visiting someone?" she asked.

"No," he said, before realizing his mistake. "I mean, yes."

"Oh? Which patient? I know them all."

Charon swore to himself. "Um, not in this ward. In another. I thought I recognized you, so…"

Her smile left her face, and her eyes widened. "You followed me?"

He was at a loss. Why did she seem upset that he would follow her? "I mean you no harm."

"Is there something I can do for you?" The friendliness had left her voice, and now she was nothing but business-like. Her unwitting prayer to him was this: *I should have known your generous gift would come at a price.*

Charon tried to think quickly for some excuse that might be acceptable to this mortal woman. "I, I'm new to town, you see. Visiting a sick relative. And, when I saw you, I thought maybe you…"

"Yes?" She frowned.

"I thought maybe you might recommend a good restaurant for dinner," he finally said.

She seemed relieved. "What kind of food do you like?"

"Greek," he said.

"George's on South Figueroa," she said. "It's not far from the hotel."

He tipped his hat. "Thank you, Matilda."

"You're welcome, sir."

He turned and left, feeling relieved that things hadn't gone worse than they had. Nonetheless, the encounter had been somewhat of a disaster, and he realized more than ever how impossible Thanatos's task of finding a companion would be.

He left the hospital and headed in the direction of his hotel. On the corner of the next block, a black dog greeted him. The animal reminded Charon of Cerberus when he was a pup—except, of course, this animal had only one head. Charon stroked the dog behind its pointed ears.

"Hello, there," Charon said as he petted the dog. "What are you doing here in the big city?"

"Starving," the dog replied with a bark.

"I have no food," Charon said. "But I can get you some."

Charon looked down one side of the street and then the other, realizing he was hungry, too. Noticing a sign in Greek, he headed that way. The dog followed him. It wasn't George's, but it would have to do.

"Your dog isn't allowed in here," a worker inside the restaurant complained.

"He's not my animal," Charon said. Then to the dog he said, "Wait outside."

A few minutes later, Charon returned to the street with a chicken kabob. He fed half of it to the dog and ate half of it himself.

"You're very generous," the dog said. "No one's ever been this kind to me."

Standing there on the curb, Charon asked, "Where do you live? Alone here on the streets? Or do you have a family?"

"I live with a cruel master who beats and starves me," the dog said. "Last night, I barely escaped with my life."

"I'm sorry to hear that," Charon said.

"You're the first person to understand me," the dog said.

Charon laughed. "That's because I'm a god, but don't let on you know."

"Why are you here, in this city?" the dog asked. "I thought gods lived in heaven."

Two men in business suits walked passed, so Charon waited until they were out of earshot to continue speaking with the dog.

"My master, Hades, sent me here for adventures," Charon said in a low voice as he squatted near the ground to pet the dog. "So, I best be off. Good luck, my friend."

Charon turned away from the dog and continued down the street.

"Wait," the dog barked, following behind.

Charon turned.

"Take me with you," the dog said.

"I'm afraid that's not possible. Go on, now."

"Please!" the dog barked.

Charon rolled his eyes and turned to face the dog. What had he gotten himself into? Was this his reward for being nice? "Look, you need to go your way, and I'll go mine. You're free now. You can do anything."

"I want to go with *you*," the dog insisted.

"You don't know what you're asking," Charon said. "I'm leaving the city—for a while anyway. A boat is no place for an animal."

Charon turned and continued down the street, but he could sense the dog following him. He sighed and tried to ignore him.

He went a few more blocks, searching for a pub, where he might have a chance at striking up a conversation. When he turned a corner, he caught a glimpse of the dog still following a few yards behind him.

Charon stopped, turned, and frowned at the dog, who was now a few feet away. "What do you want from me?"

"A friend," the dog said. "I have none."

Charon paused and wiped his brow. He understood how it felt to be alone in the world. Maybe he should give the dog a chance to be a friend to him. The animal was certainly an improvement on the human race. "I can't promise you won't be sorry."

"I'll take my chances, if it's alright with you," the dog replied.

"Follow me," Charon said, hoping he wouldn't regret it.

The dog wagged his tail and trotted happily beside him as Charon made his way down the street, looking for a private place to summon Thanatos. Charon turned down an alleyway and prayed to the god of Death.

Moments later, Thanatos appeared.

"I've found my companion," Charon said.

Than looked at the animal.

"I want to go on adventures, too," the dog barked.

Than crossed his arms and cocked his head to one side. "This wasn't what I had in mind."

"You said to make a friend, and I did," the ferryman argued.

The dog licked Charon's hand.

"What's your name?" Than asked the dog.

"Bill," the animal replied.

Thanatos turned to Charon. "You're already anxious to abandon the city for your boat on a river?"

Charon thought of Matilda, but quickly realized he couldn't attract her attention in his current condition. To her, he was an old man.

"Yes," Charon said. "Put us on a river not far from here, where we can enjoy what this world has to offer without having to bother with people."

Than arched a brow. "Not far from here? Why?"

"No reason," Charon lied. He didn't want to go too far away from Matilda. But why? He barely knew her. "For the sake of convenience."

"Fine," Than agreed. "You'll need different clothes—blue jeans and work boots, and a jacket, too, I suppose."

Charon was pleased to get out of shopping when his pants and shirt were soon replaced with proper work clothes.

Bill barked his approval. "When do we go?"

Before Charon could reply, he found himself standing on a skiff—only slightly larger than his own—on a wide river. Bill stood in front of him at the bow, glancing around in surprise.

"What the what?" Bill barked. "How did we get here?"

"Thank Death," Charon replied.

Chapter Three

The temperature was decidedly cooler as Charon steered the boat in the narrow channel through a rock archway and out into a wide expanse of water. Bill didn't seem bothered by the chill in the air, as his tail wagged happily. On each bank, the trees and shrubs, still holding onto their leaves, were vibrant golds, oranges, and tans. The sky above was clear and breathtakingly beautiful. Charon had never seen it so blue.

"Tell me about your life," Charon said, missing his ability to see the lives of the souls entering the Underworld.

"There's not much to tell," Bill said from the bow, his tail no longer wagging. "It was all so confusing."

"What do you mean?"

A bird flew overhead, screeching a peculiar song, and they were momentarily distracted by it.

Then Bill said, "I was born in a cage and lived with my mother and brothers and sisters for a short while. I was happy enough, until my master came and took me to his house. My life went downhill from there."

"What happened?" Charon wanted the details.

Bill sat back on his haunches. "At first he was nice to me. I was terrified. I didn't want to leave my family, especially my mother." Bill swiped at a tear. "But he comforted me. That first day, he doted on me."

"What changed?"

"Like I said, it was all so confusing. I could never figure out what he expected of me. He was an emotional man. I soon put it together that he'd recently lost someone he loved. I think it was his wife. I think I made him happy, at first." Bill lay on his belly and rested his snout on the boat. "I wish that day hadn't ended."

"When did he begin to beat you?" Charon asked.

"That very first day," Bill said. "I didn't know where I should relieve myself, so I found a corner in his small townhome. I thought it was out of the way and was a good choice, but he felt differently."

"You were just a pup. How could you know?"

Bill nodded. "I tried another spot, and another."

"And nothing pleased him."

"Exactly." Bill stood up, circled around, and sat back down. "After a few days of this madness, I began to understand that he wanted me to do it in the small side-yard he shared with his neighbor."

"Did things improve for you then?"

"They would have if my master had let me out often enough. He'd fall asleep for hours and hours. He drank and passed out at all hours of the day. What was I to do?"

Charon could see Bill's predicament.

"And, worst of all, it was never clear to me what was mine and what was his."

"Why was that a problem?" Charon asked, noticing a group of but-terflies scattering from one of the shrubs on the closest bank.

"He bought me toys, in those first few months. Even though he screamed at me, beat me, and, on one occasion, threw me across the room, he still had moments of kindness back then. He gave me ropes to tug on, squeaky toys to fetch, and cute little stuffed animals to rip apart. He left them scattered on the floor for me. One morning, I thought he'd given me his shoes, because he left them beside my toys on the floor. I was so excited, and I ripped one of them with pleasure. That's when he chained me to the stake in the side yard. He never let me into the house again."

"That hardly seems fair," Charon said. "It was your master's fault for leaving his shoes with your toys."

"He barely spent time with me after that. I lived for a very long time chained to the stake. My master brought me scraps to eat each evening, and I had a moldy bowl of water beneath a leaking faucet. I was forced to sit and lie down in my own waste. The only time he moved me was when it rained. I used to pray for rain, because I was then taken to the covered patio and tied to a post. It was a pleasant change from the nasty yard."

"No wonder you stink," Charon said.

"My master complained of that, too," Bill said, dropping his head with shame.

"I meant no offense, Bill," Charon quickly added, patting the dog on the head. "I don't mind it at all. And it's not your fault he never bathed you."

"There was no place to clean myself. To be honest, my smell offends even me."

"There's a simple solution to your problem," Charon said as he waved his hand toward the river.

"The river?" Bill cowered down and looked up at Charon with frightened eyes.

"Have you never been swimming?" Charon asked. It was the one thing Charon enjoyed as much as steering his boat. From time to time, he'd leap into the Acheron River and swim until he'd exhausted himself. Not often, but occasionally, Cerberus had been allowed to join him.

"I've never been anywhere but that nasty side yard," Bill explained. "Until today, when you found me after I'd escaped."

"Let's find someplace to dock." Charon directed the boat toward the nearest bank, which was still covered in brilliantly colored trees and shrubs. There was no sign of human life for miles. "This should do."

When the boat bumped against the shore, Charon climbed into the shallow water and pulled the skiff onto the grassy embankment.

Charon stripped from his clothes and tossed them into the boat. "From what I understand, dogs are natural swimmers."

The ferryman eased back into the cold water and waded out until he was chest deep.

"Come on, Bill!" Charon called.

He watched as the dog screwed up his courage.

"It's okay, boy!" Charon reassured him. "You can do it!"

Bill wagged his tail and flung himself into the water. When he emerged, he was shivering and struggling to stay afloat.

"Paddle to me," Charon said. "Just a few more yards."

Bill kept his gaze fixed on Charon as he struggled toward him in the water with a determined look on his face.

"Almost!" Charon cheered him on. "You're nearly here!"

When Bill was about two feet away, Charon reached out his arms and scooped the dog into an embrace. "You did it! Good boy, Bill!"

Bill wagged his tail eagerly, but he was as cold to the touch as the water, and he was shivering, his teeth chattering.

"Poor boy," Charon cooed, holding the dog close to his chest as he returned to the bank. "Let's get you warm and dry as soon as possible."

The ferryman stepped into his trousers and then used his jacket to dry the dog as best he could. Bill continued to shiver, so Charon held him close, using his body heat to warm him.

"I shouldn't have suggested it," Charon said regretfully. "I'd forgotten how intolerant mortals are of extreme temperatures."

"It was fun," Bill chirped through chattering teeth. "And I learned how to swim."

Charon rubbed the dog's wet coat, trying to create more heat. "Indeed. You should be proud."

When the dog continued to shiver despite Charon's efforts to warm him, Charon had an idea. Hemera, his sister and the goddess of daytime, whom he hadn't seen for centuries, might be able to help. He wrapped Bill tightly in the jacket and left him in the back of the boat. Then he stood up and called out for his sister.

She appeared before him in a halo of sunshine. "Why, I can't believe my eyes!"

"It's good to see you, too," Charon said.

"How did you escape your prison?" she asked.

Charon shook his head. "How many times have I told you and Aether that I love my job? The Underworld is my home."

"It's hard to believe that the three of us were cut from the same cloth—Aether being the upper air and I being daylight. How can you possibly be happy where the sun never shines?"

"You forget who our parents are," Charon said dryly.

"I never forget that," she said less cheerfully.

"I called you here because I need your help," Charon said.

Hemera crossed her arms and frowned. "I should have known it wasn't to be reunited with me. Charon! We haven't seen each other for ages!"

"I would have eventually come to see you, Sister," he said. "But I wanted to be in better form first."

"You look fabulous. What do you mean? You look much better than you did the last time I saw you."

He explained what Apollo had seen—why Charon had aged while the other gods had maintained their youth.

"Oh, I see," she said. "Well you look beautiful already. Distinguished even."

"Is that another way of saying I still look old?" Charon teased.

"What do you need from me, Brother?" Hemera asked, avoiding his question.

"Can you ask Helios to shine brightly on my dog? He's freezing, and I can't seem to warm him."

"Oh, you sweet thing!" Hemera said, embracing the animal that had been lying in the back of the boat. "I didn't see you there in the folds of my brother's coat."

Hemera lifted her arm into the sky and reached all the way up to where the sun god sat in his golden cup, flying across the clouds. Then she drew her arm back in to its original size as she cupped a flame in her hand.

"This should warm you," she said to the dog.

In a few moments, the dog's fur was dry.

"I can't thank you enough," Bill barked. "I feel much better. Clean and warm."

"You smell better, but not good," Charon said. "More like a river rat than a sewer, and that's progress, I suppose."

"Charon!" Hemera scolded.

"He's right," Bill said. "At least it's an improvement."

"You should take him down the Mississippi to La Crosse, to a hotel, and give him a proper bath," Hemera suggested, handing Bill over to Charon. "You both look like you could use a good meal as well."

"What do you say, Bill?" Charon asked the dog.

Bill barked his approval and wagged his tail.

"Hurry, because our mother will be coming to shoo me away, and Helios is already ahead of me, on his way to the other side of the world," Hemera added.

"Who's your mother?" Bill barked.

"Night," Charon said. "Also known as Nyx."

"Don't you want to see her?" Bill asked. "If I had a chance, I'd want to see my mother."

Charon scratched Bill behind the ears. "My mother isn't accessible anymore."

"Anymore?" Bill repeated.

"She once lived in Tartarus, in the Underworld, my home."

"As did I," Hemera explained. "And even then, we never saw each other. As soon as I flew home to Tartarus, she left to roam the Upperworld with our father. And when she came home, I took my leave. We never got along."

"She likes to have her way," Charon added. "That's why Hades made her leave Tartarus and take residence in a cave in the far east."

"Made her? I thought we escaped," Hemera said.

"I suppose it depends on who's telling the story," Charon conceded.

"It's much better this way," Hemera said. "I follow Helios, and Mother follows Selene, and their dwellings are close to ours."

"What about your father?" Bill asked.

Charon shook his head. "That's why our mother is so hard to get along with. She's either sleeping in her cave, or embracing our father, Erebus, as they fly around the world."

"I see what you meant by inaccessible," Bill laughed. "It's a wonder you don't have more brothers and sisters."

Charon chuckled and pet Bill behind the ears.

"Here comes Dusk," Hemera warned. "Better hurry." She waved. "It was good to see you."

"Likewise," Charon said. "And thanks again for your help."

As his sister flew away, Charon helped Bill into the boat and shoved off from the bank.

Charon jumped into the back of the boat as they headed south. "Now we need to get to La Crosse before nightfall."

"I thought you could see in the dark," Bill pointed out.

"I can. But the nighttime temperature this far north will be hard on you. Better to get you indoors at night until we're further south."

Bill ducked his head in shame. "I'm sorry to be a burden to you."

"Are you kidding me?" Charon laughed. "You're the best part of this trip! I'd be miserable without you."

Bill skipped up to the bow and wagged his tail with excitement, and both passengers smiled as they floated down the Mississippi beneath the falling dusk.

EVA POHLER

Eva Pohler is a *USA Today* bestselling author of over thirty novels in multiple genres, including mysteries, thrillers, and young adult paranormal romance based on Greek mythology. Her books have been described as "addictive" and "sure to thrill"—*Kirkus Reviews.*

To learn more about Eva and her books, and to sign up to hear about new releases, and sales, please visit her website at www.evapohler.com.

www.ingramcontent.com/pod-product-compliance
Lightning Source LLC
Chambersburg PA
CBHW061304210726
48293CB00003B/1112